The Dawning of the Day:
A Jerusalem Tale

Haim Sabato

THE DAWNING OF THE DAY:
A JERUSALEM TALE

Translated by

Yaacob Dweck

The Toby Press

The Toby Press LLC

First English language edition, 2006

The Dawning of the Day: A Jerusalem Tale

POB 8531, New Milford, CT. 06676-8531, USA
& POB 2455, London WIA 5WY, England
www.tobypress.com

Originally published in Hebrew as *Keafapey Shachar,* [Like the Eyelids
of Dawn] Copyright © 2004 Haim Sabato and Books in the Attic &
Miskal Publishing House Yediot Aharonot/Sifrei Hemed, Tel Aviv,

Translation © 2006 Yaacob Dweck

The right of Haim Sabato to be identified as the author
of this work has been asserted by him in accordance
with the Copyright, Designs & Patents Act 1988

Cover Artwork by Nachum Gutman,
courtesy of the Gutman Museum, Tel Aviv

ISBN I 59264 140 7, *hardcover*

A CIP catalogue record for this title is available
from the British Library Printed

Printed and bound in the United States
by Thomson-Shore Inc., Michigan

The innocence of the upright will guide them.

My great-uncle was one of the most pure-minded men of old Jerusalem. Many times I sat before him with bundles of questions in my hand. My soul burning I used to come to him with questions about the conduct of life and the ways of the world. He would answer patiently: "I shall recount to you a tale of one of the natives of Jerusalem." When he finished the tale, he smiled silently. Through the tale my problem would be solved. Once I came to him with a particular question, and he responded, as was his wont, "I shall recount a tale of one of the natives of Jerusalem, Ezra Siman Tov. It is good to tell the tale of Ezra Siman Tov," he said. I saw that as he mentioned the name his eyes lit up. My great-uncle rested his head in his hands and closed his eyes, looking like someone immersed in his memories. Several moments later he opened his eyes again; they were dark and sad. He let out a deep sigh. He was silent for another moment, and said, almost to himself, "Yes, I shall recount the tale of Ezra Siman Tov, the entire story, what his friends did for him, the tragedy of his daughter that shook all Jerusalem, and I shall recount the pain, the pain that fills the heart and threatens to break it." He was silent and bent his head. Suddenly his eyes lit up again and he smiled. He gazed at me and said: "It is good, truly good to tell the story of Ezra Siman Tov."

Chapter one

In which we recount Ezra's tale.

Ezra Siman Tov was a man of Jerusalem who lived by the labor of his own hands, like those of whom it is said, "Greater is the man who lives by the sweat of his own brow than the man who fears heaven." No title preceded his name. People did not call him Haham Ezra or Señor Ezra. He was simply Ezra. Day after day Ezra Siman Tov rose early, happily going to work and returning home. He was not like those of whom it was said, "When he has a hundred, he wants two hundred," but rather, "Who is rich? He who is content with his lot."

He was early to rise, and early to bed. He had heard a wonderful homily by Haham Yosef Pinto one Sabbath on the verse: *How long wilt thou sleep, O sluggard? When wilt thou arise out of thy sleep?* How long will a sluggard lie in bed? And should you ask, "What does it matter?" Scripture responds, *When wilt thou arise out of thy sleep?* Ezra was not one of the lazy ones, one who turned his days into nights and nights into days, rising from his slumber like a prince at nine o'clock, three hours after the day had dawned, not going to sleep until midnight; one who complains that the Holy One, Blessed be He, orders the world incorrectly, because not only does He cause the sun to set at the height of the day, but He also causes it to rise three hours before one should awaken, thus squandering three hours of sunlight. If the world were in their hands, the sun would set at midnight and rise at nine o'clock. Ezra was not one to complain. He was happy in the world of the Holy One, Blessed be He, very happy. One of those about whom they said, "good for Heaven, good for the creatures." Were his name not already Siman Tov*, it would have been fitting to call him so.

This was his habit. He rose at dawn. Readied himself, drank a cup of tea, wrapped himself in a fringed prayer shawl, donned tefillin, and walked at a slow measured pace on the path to the synagogue. Outside, morning dew settled on the ground, and he inhaled the pure air of Jerusalem. Sweet was the air; he would not have exchanged it for anywhere else in the world. As he walked, the morning blessings surfaced on his lips, each one vying to be his first utterance. Were Ezra not restrained by nature, all the blessings would have emerged at the same time: *Blessed is He who gives strength to the weak, Blessed is He who sets the crooked straight, Blessed is He who has provided for all my needs.* It was obvious that each blessing gave him great joy. As he stretched his limbs he recited: *He who gives sight to the blind may His name be blessed. He who frees the imprisoned may His name be blessed.* In his mind he remembered Haham Pinto's interpretation of the verse, *Wherefore doth a living man complain?* It is enough that he is alive. He hummed the verses composed by the poet for the blessing, *He who restores the souls of the dead,* to the tune of the dawn hymns sung on the Sabbath: *You have found it renewed, with additions, and improved, like a bride adorned, morning after morning; in His promise ever loyal, restore me to my toil, man expires not in his sin, it was evening and it was morning.* After the morning blessings, he used to say, "Now I intend to fulfill the precept to love my neighbor as myself and shall love each member of the house of Israel as my own flesh." This tradition he had received from his father, Nissim Melamed Siman Tov,

---

* Lit. Good Omen; Good Symbol

who had received it from his father, Haham Ya'akob Bava Melamed Siman Tov Ghurni.

Usually, Ezra had not finished reciting the blessings when he arrived at the synagogue. He prayed with the dawn minyan of the Zoharei Hamah Synagogue in Mahane Yehudah in Jerusalem. There were about twenty men who regularly attended the service. They had an extraordinary cantor, Haham Elijah Raful. He was called Elijah HaMekhaven, Elijah the Diviner, for two reasons: he knew how to divine the names and how to ascertain the time. Divining the names I cannot explain to you, for I do not engage in the mystical secrets; but I can explain what it means to discover the time. He timed the blessings so that the *Shema* coincided exactly with sunrise, in order to fulfill the verse in Scripture, *They shall fear thee as long as the sun endures.* Elijah HaMekhaven was not one of those cantors about whom it was said, *It crieth out against me: therefore have I hated it,* but rather, *let me see thy countenance, let me hear thy voice; for sweet is thy voice, and thy countenance is comely.* His voice was deep but pleasing. Very pleasing for the dawn services in the Zoharei Hamah Synagogue in Mahane Yehudah in Jerusalem. Their dawn service was not like the dawn service held on Shavuot, the Feast of Weeks, when congregations stay awake the entire night in order to repair the sin of our biblical ancestors who were sleeping in their tents when the Holy One, Blessed be He, wanted to give them the Torah at Sinai. Such congregations want to pray at dawn, but they are not accustomed to it, and are unable to decipher the precise time. Their cantor ascends to the pulpit, watch in hand, sets it down before him and prays, one eye on the prayer book, the other on his watch. At first the congregants hurry him along, then they slow him down; he draws out the passages he should shorten and shortens those he should lengthen; and nevertheless, he misses the precise moment of sunrise. This was not the way of Elijah HaMekhaven. At Zoharei Hamah they were accustomed to praying at dawn, and Elijah HaMekhaven prayed as he usually did without so much as a glance at his watch. When he recited the blessing, *He who redeemed Israel,* immediately before the silent prayer, they would rise just as the sun appeared on the horizon.

It seemed as if the sun had already spread its red canopy over the east and was ready to appear in all its glory, but was waiting for Elijah HaMekhaven to finish reciting *He who redeemed Israel.*

At this hour Ezra used to open the Synagogue window and gaze at the sunrise, his lips reciting the prayer, *Creator of light, creator of darkness, maker of peace, maker of all things.* Thus it was every day. His prayer was never rushed, but steady and measured. He was not one of those who waited with bated breath to hear the cantor recite, *And the Redeemer shall come to Zion,* immediately removing his tefillin and folding his prayer shawl, standing before God stripped naked of His mitzvot, one foot in the synagogue, the other in the street, quickly mumbling, *They Shall Bless Him* and *We Shall Praise Him,* the final two passages of the morning service, on their way out, as if they were the traveler's prayer. Ezra was not one of the hasty ones. He stood wrapped in his prayer shawl, crowned with his tefillin until the end of the service, lingering, reciting *Surely the righteous shall give thanks unto thy name* or other verses that attest to God's mercy, then he would sit down next to the long table, a volume of the *Hok L'Yisrael* open before him, reading the daily portion. Always he read the daily selection from that Sabbath's scriptural reading, its Aramaic translation, one Mishnah with Ovadiah of Bertinoro's commentary, two short paragraphs of Maimonides' code, and a few ethical teachings from *The Pele Yo'etz.* He understood whatever he could, and what he could not, he felt in his heart.

This study of the *Hok L'Yisrael,* while wrapped in his prayer shawl and crowned with his tefillin, drew a thread of grace over Ezra Siman Tov that he would not have exchanged for all the wealth in the world. The days he did not finish his reading did not count for him as genuine days. In his volume he placed little slips of paper with the names of the sick in need of prayer; on the inside cover he recorded the names of his children and the times of their births:

> My son Nissan born amid great joy on Tuesday, a day doubly blessed by God at Creation, the first day of the glorious month of Adar.

At dawn the morning following Gedaliah's Fast, my daughter Rebecca was born, under a good omen, shining like the sun.

My son Raphael, may he live under God's protection, was born at twilight, on the Sabbath eve, at an auspicious hour, on the week whose portion contained, '*I will put none of these diseases upon thee, which I have brought upon the Egyptians: for I am the Lord that healeth thee.*' And he fell ill but was saved by the Doctor Yeshiah Mattiyah, a messenger of God, may his name be remembered for the good.

Next to these inscriptions was an image of the Menorah formed by the words of the sixty-seventh Psalm, a charm against wicked forces. In the verses he read in the *Hok L'Yisrael,* he discovered allusions to his affairs for the coming day, perhaps a sign for his success. If he had committed a sin, he discerned an allusion to it in one of the verses he read, and immediately his thoughts turned to repentance.

During this hour, while reading, Ezra would be approached by the charity collectors of Jerusalem. Not the collectors that you know. There are charity collectors in Jerusalem not known to all. They neither approach everyone nor appeal on behalf of just anybody. They are modest collectors who approach humble folk on behalf of the deserving poor. The old Jerusalem scholars know who these are, and send them to those in genuine need. When they approach their particular donors, they speak briefly and allusively without urgency or argument. So too with Ezra. They would greet him briefly, "Good morning Ezra. An unassuming orphaned bride. A learned scholarly groom. Your share is twenty lira." Or they would say, "Good morning Ezra. Can we offer you a share in one of God's precepts? A businesses man has lost his fortune. It is better to leave his name unsaid. Your Honor's portion is fifty lira." And he would reach into his wallet without a word, take out money and give it to them. "May you be worthy to fulfill the precepts, Ezra."

"May you be worthy to fulfill them as well," he would respond, returning to his reading.

Each day when he finished his reading he went home. Jaffa Road on his return from prayer was nothing like on his way to prayer. The same road that had accompanied his steps to the synagogue in silence and listened to his recitation of the morning blessings in tranquility was bustling with activity. People hurrying to work, rushing and running. The morning warmth had replaced the coolness of dawn, and the world in which Ezra had walked alone was now filled with people. At his home, breakfast was already waiting. In the winter, a cup of warm *Sahlep*, the milk frothing on top and decorated with fine-smelling cinnamon, and a cheese *boreka* beside it. In the summer a cup of mint tea, and several *ka'ak* topped with yellow sesame seeds. His wife Madame Sarah sitting at his side reminding him as he ate where they had to go that evening; to the *Zohar* feast for her niece's newborn son, held on the eve of his circumcision, or the memorial service marking the one-year anniversary of their uncle's passing, or the *pidyon haben*, redemption of the firstborn, for Haham Bechor Atiah's grandson. Ezra did not tarry long at his house, but hurried to work. Madame Sarah watched him from the doorway of the house, kissing the mezuzah and mumbling to herself as well as to Ezra her husband, "May the Lord be with you."

Ezra worked in Yehezkel Kaduri's laundry, next to the Mahane Yehudah market. Ironing clothes was his craft. Hot vapor filled Kaduri's laundry. Ezra would take a wrinkled garment in his hand straight from the laundry, smooth it out, and look upon it, as if to say: You have seen better days, days when you were purchased for a young woman's engagement or for Passover Eve. Slowly you descended from your place of the highest honor. At first they began to wear you on the Sabbath. When your beauty had faded you began to be worn on a regular weekday with pants that did not match. As he was looking at it he would smooth out the folds on the jacket and stroke it soothingly, as if to say: Such is the way of the world. A verse from Ecclesiastes he had once heard in Haham Pinto's Sabbath sermon would occur to him: *In the day of prosperity be joyful, but in the day of adversity consider: God also hath set the one over against the other, to the end that man should find nothing after him.* He who recognizes that the riches in his life are not his own shall not be defiant a single day longer. The earth is the Lord's and He governs it thus, may His name be blessed. Day after day, from the morning prayers until the afternoon prayers Ezra stood on his feet, flattening pleats, straightening creases, and ironing them so the garment would be smooth.

Ezra was not numbered among those whose craft was easy, or among those whose craft was shameful. His craft allowed him to earn his keep. People respected him as they saw fit. Ezra did not pursue glory, nor did glory tire itself out chasing after him. On days when people paid him too much respect, he worried. It was a tradition that if a person received greater respect than his due, the day would come when he received greater shame than his due. He had once received good advice from Haham Yosef Pinto: If people give a man too much honor he should not resist but store up the spare honor; at another time, when he thinks they are not giving him his due, he should turn to the treasury of honor to restore his peace of mind.

An hour before sunset he would finish his work and take his leave of the owner. "Peace, blessing, and goodness, Yehezkel. Sleep in peace." Always this same formulation. There are many greetings in Jerusalem; each one has its specific time and place. The greeting upon meeting a friend differs from the one recited upon departure; the one in the morning differs from the one in the evening; those on festivals differ from those offered during a normal weekday. The one greeted also knows the proper response. If someone wishes him, "sleep in peace" he responds "awake in great mercy"; if someone blesses him on a festival by saying, "may you merit many years," he replies, "may you merit a long life, may your days extend." To the blessing, "A peaceful Sabbath," he responds, "Peace and good blessing"; to "Good morning," he says, "to the master as well"; to "Bless Him who heals the sick," "may He and His name be blessed"; to "Welcome," "welcome to those who greet us." In short, from the way a man greets his fellow man, one can tell if he is a native of Jerusalem. Where Ezra and his fellow residents of Jerusalem learned all these different greetings

I do not know. Some they certainly learned from their teachers, of blessed memory; as for those that were silent, their faces indicated if they were Jerusalem natives.

After he took his leave from work, Ezra took two baskets and went to the Mahane Yehudah market. Ezra Siman Tov purchased all his fruits and vegetables in the Mahane Yehudah market, according to Jerusalem custom. Some people love to ramble through forests and streams in the wilderness, others in great towns and ancient cities. Ezra Siman Tov loved to stroll through the Mahane Yehudah market among the stands for fruits and vegetable, chickens and spices. The stall owners all knew him and he knew them as well, natives of Jerusalem like him. "Peace be upon you, Ezra." "Peace, blessing, and goodness." The big market and the little market, the Iraqi alley and the Kurdish alley, he knew them all. The colorful array of the red tomatoes and the green peppers, the black eggplants and yellowish pears laid out on the stalls in heaps or in towers; the Arab peddler women in their black dresses embroidered with colorful patches next to mounds of fresh onions that were still covered with the soil of the field; the narrow baskets of figs, plucked from the tree at dawn and stewing in their sweetness; the pungent odors of coriander and black pepper; the coffee grinder releasing the intoxicating smell of ground coffee beans; the shelf filled with sweets made by Havilio, sparkling in all their different colors; the red heads of the cocks butting out of giant crates and screaming for salvation; small stalls with brown beans, yellowish chickpeas, red lentils next to rolls of rope whose use no one knows; the deep voices of the stall owners hawking their wares in the tune used to recite the Mishnah—all this entranced Ezra. Every day he went shopping in the market, whether or not he needed anything. Such was his custom, the custom of Jerusalem.

Several moments before sunset Ezra would arrive at the Zoharei Hamah Synagogue for the afternoon service. He would put down his overflowing baskets underneath the bench and wash his hands, and open with the Psalm, *How amiable are thy tabernacles, O Lord of hosts! My soul longeth, yea even fainteth for the courts of the Lord: my heart and my flesh crieth out for the living God.* Slowly, slowly he would recite

them. Following the afternoon service he would remain in the synagogue, joining Haham Menashe Kahanof's class on *The Ben Ish Hai*,
the great book of laws by the Baghdadi rabbi, Yosef Haim. Occasionally his head drooped down from the day's exhaustion and he dozed
off. Such was his custom from Sundays through Thursdays.

Chapter two

In which we take leave of Ezra nodding off in Rabbi Kahanof's class and recount the story of the writer and what he told Ezra.

There once was a great writer in Jerusalem. All Jerusalem took pride in him, both during his life and after his death. His fame extended throughout the world. He wrote many stories; tales of pain, tales of anguish, tales which appeared humorous until the anguish emerged, old tales, even older tales, and tales which renewed themselves daily; tales whose end came at the beginning and tales which evolved as they were written. Many people eagerly awaited the appearance of each new story. Scholars, in their attempt to understand his every word, split hairs like yeshiva students. At times, they offered sound explanations; at others, only casuistry.

Until the beginnings of a story appeared to him, the writer suffered great anguish. Who could understand the writer's pain, as his spirit raged and stormed like a river threatening to flow over its banks? Wrestling in his mouth, words struggled to set themselves free. His pen produced gem after gem, but he lacked even the slightest thread upon which to string them. Although he possessed much, he thought himself a pauper. In his own eyes he was more destitute than all the poor. They had absolutely nothing; he had many coins and yearned to use them but could not. Woe is he who has a palace but holds not the key! Such was the nature of those treasures: they could not reveal themselves unless they were suspended on a thread that could bear them all. The simpler the thread, the greater the weight it could bear. But for all its simplicity, it escaped the very wealthy and was found only among the poor. In truth this thread could be found among all. So much treasure glitters before the rich that they cannot discern it because of its simplicity. The poor, who have nothing, delight in it and adorn themselves with it.

What would the writer do in those moments of anguish? At times, he searched the introductions to old books or combed through leaflets he had around the house, collections of Hasidic tales or anthologies of ancient rabbinic legends. In these stories he might find something. At times, he wandered through Jerusalem and asked simple folk to accompany him; perhaps while walking he might hear that one story. At times, he invited himself to an Ashkenazi *shteeble* in Me'ah She'arim between the afternoon and evening prayers, or to the Sephardi synagogue in the Bukharan Quarter. He listened attentively to the sermons of the preachers in the study house and the conversations of the worshippers as they emerged from the synagogue for a breath of fresh air. Usually, the writer returned home empty-handed and his anguish only increased. Yet occasionally he was the beneficiary of a kindness; the simple story of an elderly man would suddenly ignite a spark, and he would realize, I have story. He would clutch the thread and refuse to release it. If the old man in the synagogue only knew what a treasure he possessed. It lay concealed within him, but the writer took it, filed it, polished it, refined it, and hung pearls on it until it gleamed in many shades.

At times, on his walks, the writer would happen upon the Zoharei Hamah Synagogue in Mahane Yehudah. He might hear a parable from Haham Pinto, a noteworthy story from Haham Zion Ventura, the Spaniard, or an insight from Haham Menashe Kahanof in his class on *The Ben Ish Hai*. Once, as he left the synagogue empty-handed, he emerged pensive and weary. As he walked, he noticed a man with a shining face in the alley near the entrance to the synagogue. The man stood encircled by a group of people who were listening to him with rapt attention. The writer too began to listen and his eyes lit up. He had found it. An actual story.

The man was recounting a story he had heard from a certain Hasid at a meal one Sabbath afternoon in Zikhron Kedoshim Synagogue. This was the story he told: Rabbi Zvi, the spiritual leader of the Jews of Zhidachov, was once approached by his congregants on the holiday of Purim. They were joking, dressed up in the clothing worn by ministers at court. His nephew even appeared before him dressed as the prime minister. All were drunk on wine. Rabbi Zvi treated them like royalty and paid them great respect. He pleaded and entreated them to enact a royal decree annulling both the candle tax and the royal prohibition on kosher meat. They agreed. They wrote the decree and sealed it. Then Rabbi Zvi further implored them to annul the conscription of Jewish youth into the royal army. But this the prime minister refused. The others began to press him at great length, but he continued to resist. Finally, the rabbi himself pleaded with his nephew, who was drunk on wine and dressed in a minister's fine clothing. Yet the prime minister would not consent under any circumstances. When the wine had worn off the day after Purim, the Hasidim asked him why he had refused the request of his uncle, their spiritual leader. He responded that he could not remember a thing from the day before. A short time later, the prime minister annulled the candle tax and the royal prohibition on kosher meat but maintained conscription into the royal army.

As the storyteller spoke, his eyes sparkled. The audience gathered around him in a tight ring and strained to hear his every word. The writer stood to the side; he observed the man and observed his audience. He saw the satisfaction on their faces.

That storyteller was Ezra Siman Tov.

From that day on, the writer arranged to accompany Ezra from time to time on his way home from synagogue after the evening prayer.

Most of the time they were silent, the writer out of force of habit and Ezra because he did not know what to say. Occasionally, Ezra would casually remark, "I have a story, a story I heard from Haham Ventura, a story about Haj Adoniahu, one of those forcibly converted to Islam in Meshed, Persia. Afterwards, Adoniahu escaped and was rescued. A short while later, he came to the Holy Land and built a synagogue." Or, "I have a story about the porter on Porters' Street in Jerusalem. It was rumored that Elijah had revealed himself to the porter." During Ezra's stories, the writer listened in silence.

On one occasion, they walked a long way in silence. The writer had nearly reached his own house when Ezra suddenly turned to him and remarked, "Listen to the following story. It happened fifty years ago. It is a story about four young men who were playing in a field in the neighborhood of Mahane Yehudah in Jerusalem." He began to talk, yet he did not tell the story in his usual fashion. Normally Ezra told his stories with a sweet smile on his lips, composing a story like those who ran worry-beads on their fingers, pausing between each sentence in order to allow time for reflection. This time, Ezra spoke without stopping. His voice was different, rising and falling, and occasionally even trembling. When he concluded the story, he released a pent-up sigh and fell silent. The writer, too, was silent. They continued to walk. Suddenly Ezra asked, "What do you say? How do you as a writer think this story ends? Is there any way of putting it right? Does it have a happy ending?"

The writer was silent. Ezra was silent. They continued walking. After a few moments, Ezra said, "You are a writer and compose many stories out of your own imagination. If you were to happen upon a story like this, how would you conclude it? Would you heal his pain or perhaps...." They continued walking. Ezra whispered, "Please, sir, you are a writer. A writer can write whatever occurs to him. Is that not so? After all, the story belongs to you as if it were clay in the hands of a potter. Do what you will with it. Write an end for the story. Nobody can tell you what to write with your own pen, but, for my sake, couldn't you write that...what difference would it make to you? Surely what you, as a writer, choose to write is what will be written. Is that not so, sir? Would it really be impossible for you to find a remedy for this man? Is it truly impossible, sir? Is it entirely impossible?"

Ezra fell silent. He looked at the writer, but the writer's face was impenetrable. They continued walking. The writer arrived at his house and pressed Ezra's hand without uttering a word. Ezra turned to leave. Then the writer turned and called to Ezra. He said to him, "I once heard a Hasidic story. Once, the Ba'al Shem Tov told a man who had come to him: If the day comes when you hear your own story from someone else, know that there will be a remedy." The writer turned and went on his way.

Chapter three

In which we leave the remedy for its proper time and recount what befell Doctor Yehudah Tawil at the singing of the Sabbath dawn hymns.

Ezra Siman Tov on the Sabbath was nothing like Ezra Siman Tov during the week. On Friday, Ezra finished his work before noon, as was the custom in Jerusalem, set out to the ritual bath in the Bukharan Quarter and immersed himself twice. The first time he directed his mind to purging himself of the working week, and the second time to sanctifying himself with the holiness of the Sabbath. Each time he immersed himself in the water, he meticulously ensured that it covered his entire body with no part left untouched. Upon emerging from the water after the second immersion, he dried himself and felt something akin to the Sabbath holiness. Consequently he did not even pause in the outside room, where some were naked and others clothed. As it was forbidden to speak words of Torah in such a room, the men bantered in idle gossip. They chatted about the land and its fruit, the upkeep of the synagogue and the business of the Sephardi council, news of the war and the price of stocks and shares. Ezra, who had already sanctified himself, paid no attention to what was said in that room. He nodded his head to some of his neighbors, taking care not to greet anyone with the word "peace" while in the bathhouse. For Peace is one of the names of the Holy One, Blessed be He.

On leaving the ritual bath each Friday he went home. Upon arrival he would eat a small portion of rice or some beans, not to satiate himself but to silence his hunger. He wanted to begin the Sabbath with a hearty appetite, not afflicted by pains of hunger. When he entered the kitchen, he took the lids off several pots and tasted the Sabbath delicacies in order to fulfill the precept *those who taste it merit eternal life.* After taking a short nap, he awoke while he could still see the light of day. He donned his Sabbath garb and began to recite the weekly portion with the Aramaic translation. The entire house was astir. His wife, Madame Sarah, was cleaning and washing, baking and seasoning, yet he seemed secluded in another world. Sitting in his Sabbath dress, he chanted the weekly portion with the Aramaic translation. Several times Ezra had tried to persuade his children to sit down with him and join him in the recitation, but he had not succeeded. His children, they did things a different way. Hastening, hurrying, rushing. Yet in spite of all this, they would still arrive at synagogue late, in the middle of the hymn *Come O Beloved to greet the Sabbath bride.*

From the moment Ezra donned his Sabbath attire it was as if he were clothed in royalty. On every other day of the week, he wore a brown cap and faded dull clothing, the dress of a tradesman in Jerusalem, but on the Sabbath he wore a finely pressed white shirt and a dark suit and crowned his head with a black silk hat, as if he were Señor Eliachar from the Sephardi council rather than Ezra Siman Tov. Well before the sun had set, he took his prayer book in hand and slowly made his way to the Western Wall to recite the Song of Songs and greet the Sabbath bride. Who could compare to him? Who could possibly measure up to him during those moments when he stood by the Western Wall? As the sun sank, the west blushed and a throng of white doves hovered with fluttering wings. A reddish hue cloaked Jerusalem, and a wondrous silence descended upon the city. At that hour a particular grace spread throughout the city and one of its threads hung above Ezra Siman Tov. And he chanted the sweet melody of the Song of Songs, *Because of the savour of thy good ointments thy name is as ointment poured forth, therefore do the virgins love thee. Draw me, we will run after thee.* As the minyan was gathering and the sun was setting, they would all turn to the west to greet the Sabbath with the song written by Solomon Alkabetz. *Brush yourself off, arise from the dust, renew yourself from the earth. Rise up and clothe yourself in your glory.* And what are the clothes of your glory? *O my nation.* For the nation of Israel is the glory of the holy city of Jerusalem. On more than one occasion, Ezra would close his eyes at that very moment and imagine the Sabbath as a bride wrapped in a veil coming towards him as he went out to greet her.

After each Friday night's prayers he walked home. He entered his house and called out "Good Sabbath." Madame Sarah would be sitting in the corner of the verandah. A white Sabbath headscarf finished with lace filigree covered her head and descended upon her shoulders. The Sabbath candles, placed in the silver candlesticks that she had inherited from her grandmother, Señora Mazal, would illuminate her face with a special splendor. When her husband greeted her, she would lower her eyes and respond, "Good and blessed Sabbath." After he had encircled the table twice, Madame Sarah would hand him two bunches of myrtle, one for each of the two biblical mitzvot, *Remember the Sabbath* and *Keep the Sabbath.* He would rub them between his hands several times until their sweet smell had mixed with the powerful scents of the plant on the windowsill and the intoxicating aroma of the jasmine climbing the garden walls. In a loud voice, he would recite *Blessed is He who creates the fragrant plants* and take his seat at the head of the table.

On the table twelve loaves of pita bread would be waiting, baked by Madame Sarah in honor of the Sabbath, as was the custom of residents of Jerusalem. The pita would be covered by a white cloth with a beautiful pattern of gold and blue threads, embroidered by Madame Sarah herself in honor of the Sabbath bride.

When Ezra began to chant the melody *Welcome unto thee,* he would concentrate his thoughts on the heavenly angels. Immediately thereafter he would sing to his wife *The Woman of Valor,* from the book of Proverbs. It seemed as if King Solomon had written this poem especially for the mistress of a house who had worked and toiled the entire day with her own hands. Ezra would sanctify the Sabbath with a blessing over the wine, and they would eat. After the meal, Madame Sarah would serve him black sunflower seeds and white pumpkin seeds that she had roasted for the Sabbath. She roasted them with great precision, taking particular care that they did not burn. As she toiled, her lips would utter a prayer for the success of her efforts, that the labor might turn out well for the sake of the holy Sabbath and in honor of Ezra, her husband, that he might enjoy them and delight in her.

After each Sabbath meal, Ezra opened the songbook and began to sing the verses of Rabbi Israel Najara:

> *My shepherd, my protector*
> *For the feet of them that mock*
> *To whom didst Thou abandon*
> *The smallest of Thy flock*
> *Thy scattered remnant gather*
> *The offspring of Thy lover*
> *And, peace bring to Thy brother*
> *Yea, peace unto Thy flock*

It was said of Rabbi Israel Najara that when he intoned his hymns, the angels would cease their singing to come and listen. Perhaps they also came to listen to Ezra Siman Tov. Those who understood allusions would interpret the verse *Each of them had six wings* as follows: Why does each angel have six wings? Because on each and every day of the week the angels fly with a different one of the six wings and recite a song. When the Sabbath comes, the angels ask one another "With what else shall we sing?" A voice from heaven emerges and says, *"from the wings of the earth have we heard songs.* Go out among the people of Israel who are sitting at their tables and singing in the secret speech of the holy Seraphs in honor of the holy Sabbath." Ezra would continue singing until his eyes began to close.

On many occasions Ezra attempted to sit his children down and teach them the Sabbath hymns, but he could never succeed. They did things differently. Immediately after the meal, they would leave the table and stretch out on their beds to read a book. What type of book? A work in honor of the holy Sabbath? Praise of righteous men? Explanations or parables about the weekly reading? Perhaps they read a different sort of book which contained other things. Ezra did not know, and neither do I. They returned in time to recite the grace after meals, but they did not remain seated at the table. In truth, it pained Ezra greatly that they had not tasted the sweetness of the Sabbath, but he did not reveal his pain to them. If he had done so, they would have remained at the table in deference to their father. But he wanted them to sit at the table out of respect for the Sabbath. Only his wife, Madame Sarah, stayed at his side. As she listened to the hymns, she would accompany him with quiet humming or sometimes, a gentle whisper. Meanwhile, Ezra would recount to her a pleasant parable that he had heard from Haham Pinto or an acrostic from Haham Kahanof. Forty years later, when his children remembered those Sabbath evenings, they would be filled with longing, and overcome with a feeling of tenderness. But those days still lay in the distant future. Was Rabbi Pinto not fond of saying, one must wait forty years to appreciate his master's teachings? Happy is the man who appreciates what he has before it is lost.

On winter Sabbaths, from the time of the reading of the book of Genesis until the Sabbath of Remembrance shortly before Purim, the days were short and the nights long. Ezra would rise before sunrise to sing the dawn hymns. Slowly he would walk in the darkness through the alleyways of Mahane Yehudah to the Ades Synagogue. The sky was always studded with stars and the streets silent and empty. An excursion through the streets of Jerusalem after midnight on the Sabbath was a foretaste of the world to come. As he continued through the streets, he would begin to anticipate the poems of the dawn hymns, one after the other. Words laden with emotion, melodies filled with longing. As Ezra entered the synagogue he would pause, kiss the mezuzah, and recite: *As for me, I will come into Thy house in the abundance of Thy mercy.* He would bow slightly and complete the verse, *And in Thy fear will I worship toward Thy holy Temple.* Six or seven members of the synagogue would have already arrived. As he made his way to his usual place, they would raise themselves slightly from their seats and nod their heads in greeting. Haim Mizrahi, the beadle, would exclaim in a warm voice, "Ezra Siman Tov, Good Sabbath! A fair Sabbath, Ezra," as if he were an usher announcing the guests at an evening ball.

The synagogue would begin to fill up with elders, youths and children. Every time someone entered the sanctuary, all would rise from their seats and nod their heads in honor of the new arrival. Here was Rabbi David Ma'aravi, a man of afflictions, who had lost his leg when it was hit by shrapnel as he was fetching water during the riots, who entered leaning on his cane; Haham Natan Salem, the pious Syrian mystic, a handsome bearded man; Rabbi Shabbtai Bibi of Safed, clutching an embroidered colorful cushion on which to sit; Haham Yosef Hadad, the Djerban, with little bags full of multicolored candies made by Havilio for the children.

Haim Mizrahi, the aged beadle, would already be passing through with glasses of mint tea and a plate of sweet dates on a sparkling brass tray. Each man would take a glass of tea and recite out loud in a clear voice, *Blessed is He for all was created through His word.* Everyone would respond after him, *Amen.* Haim Mizrahi knew them all. He remembered who took his tea with lemon and who took it with a stick of cinnamon; who drank sweet tea and who was not allowed to have even the slightest bit of sugar. Each and every one of them received his proper portion.

In the meantime the cantors would begin to arrive. Those who actually were cantors, those training to become cantors, and those who thought of themselves as cantors but certainly were not. They would begin to sing the dawn hymns. Some of the dawn hymns the congregation sang together, others they sang in two groups, and still others the cantors performed individually. Each one would wait his turn to demonstrate his vocal virtuosity. While each feigned deference for his colleagues, he would really be waiting for them to ask him to sing the new melody he had heard and adapted to the words of the dawn hymns. For the entire week each cantor would prepare himself for this one moment. Thus he would pay close attention to the elder cantors and examine their faces in an effort to detect glows of satisfaction or sniffs of scorn.

Among those listening to the dawn hymns was Ezra Siman Tov's great brother-in-law, the brother of Madame Sarah, that very same respected man of letters and scholar of poetry, Doctor Yehudah Tawil, who had immigrated to the land of Israel from Aleppo in his youth. He had excelled in his studies at the Hebrew University and now gloried in the title of his doctorate. During the singing of the dawn hymns Doctor Tawil sat off to the side. As much as he participated, he still kept himself aloof. It was if he were proclaiming that he was not actually a member of the community. He was both an insider and an outsider. He cherished the dawn hymns for their poetry. For all that he wanted to uphold the traditions of his father and his father's fathers, he was a scholar of the Hebrew poetry of Sepharad at an important university and not a simple song lover like the rest of the congregation. For they sat and sang from booklets of the dawn hymns printed in Jerusalem by the cantor Asher Mizrahi, and their primary concern was the cantor's solo and the transitions between the different musical modes. If the cantor mangled the meter or wrecked the rhyme in order to accommodate his melodic flourishes, they simply did not notice. While they clearly did not understand the words of the dawn hymns and experienced them as emotion, he sat with the great tomes of the medieval Hebrew poets published by Haim Brody in Berlin at the turn of the twentieth century. On numerous occasions, Doctor Tawil would chuckle to himself when he heard the simple souls confounding the verses of the dawn hymns. But at times he was so overcome with passion that he would rise from his seat. Enraged, he would approach them and interrupt their singing. Using the great tomes from the university he would try to show them the correct version of the hymn and exactly where they had made their mistake. They listened to him, either out of respect or to appease him and to prevent him from starting a troublesome quarrel. Everyone remembered the great dispute between him and the cantor, Nissim Dweck, about a single letter that denoted the definite article in a poem by Ibn Ezra. The cantor stubbornly refused to pronounce that one letter. Even after Doctor Tawil adduced proof upon proof from verses in the Bible, writings of the Sages, and medieval manuscripts, Cantor Dweck refused to listen to him. The cantor told him, "This is the received tradition from our fathers, and our fathers from their fathers, for many generations. We will not change our custom simply because of what you people have learned from scholars at the university." Doctor Tawil took to his feet and held to his opinion, raising his voice until all the singing for that Sabbath was thrown into disarray. Since that incident, everyone knew that one did not argue with him.

Haim Mizrahi came around the room again, this time with candies for the children and boxes of snuff tobacco for the adults. Every man would take a pinch of snuff in his hand, sniff it, extend his hand to the beadle and bring it back to his forehead as a gesture of appreciation. And then behold, Haham Pinto would arrive. The entire congregation would rise to its feet, the cantors stopping the hymn they had been singing and beginning a hymn especially in his honor: *Singular, Lord, Chief among thousands, Bless the great man, whose soul is beloved, with love and great kindness. Let us welcome him, Let us welcome him.* They always continued singing until the Haham reached his place and took his seat. He would take part in the singing of two or three hymns before rising to deliver his homily.

The homily Haham Yosef preached during the singing of the dawn hymns differed from the one he preached later on the Sabbath day. Each was a performance unto itself. During the dawn hymns, he would fill his homily with stories of redemption, expound upon parables, and compose numerologies using the letters of the Hebrew alphabet as numerals. All who listened savored the taste of the Sabbath night, the taste of mint tea and sweet dates. Each time he would tell a story about the singing of the dawn hymns. Like the tale about the exalted and pious Haham Abraham Antebi, blessed be the memory of the righteous. Once, the governor of Aleppo outlawed the singing of dawn hymns after midnight because they disturbed his sleep. Nevertheless, the exalted and righteous sage, the crown of the community, Haham Antebi, instructed the entire congregation not to be frightened or scared, but to come to the singing of the dawn hymns as was their custom. When the governor arrived and raised his hand in anger, Haham Antebi directed his mind at it until the hand withered and could not move. Only after members of the governor's household threw themselves at the Haham's feet and pleaded that he release the governor from his plight did he yield. Or he would tell the tale about Haham Ya'akob Ades, who, when people approached him to kiss his hand, would pull it back and say, "I am not worthy." His attendant, who used to walk at his side, had a handsome face and long beard. Once, someone mistook him for the Haham. He hurried to take the attendant's hand and bestow a kiss upon it. The attendant, who had accompanied Haham Ades for many years, withdrew his hand and responded, "I am not worthy." Haham Ya'akob looked at his attendant with affection and smiled. "My son, take heed," he said to him. "In your case, they will believe you...." This was how the Haham preached. Before he concluded his sermon, he would praise those in the house of Israel who renounced the pleasure of sleep and rose early during the Sabbath night to exalt their creator. Then the congregation would recite the chapter of the oral law that begins with the phrase *Rabbi Hananya* and always precedes the kaddish. They always closed with the kaddish for Israel and the Rabbis.

The cantor began the morning prayer with the customary passage from the book of Samuel, *And Hannah prayed*. After the service, Ezra returned home and ate lunch. He fulfilled the mitzvah to enjoy rest on the Sabbath. After his nap, he went to synagogue for the afternoon prayer.

On Sabbath afternoon, Ezra would pray in the synagogue of the ashkenazim, Zikhron Kedoshim, on Degel Reuven Street. Following the afternoon prayer, Ezra would eat the third meal of the Sabbath with them. Those meals tasted like no other. In the courtyard of the Zikhron Kedoshim Synagogue, a wooden board was placed atop two pairs of metal table legs. Upon the table lay a white tablecloth and ten plates. Thus it was every Sabbath; ten plates, a piece of herring on each plate, with congealed fish sauce and two black olives. Three bottles of beer, two loaves of bread, salt, and a goblet of wine for the grace after meals adorned the table. A minyan of ten Jewish men sat upon stools without backs. *A Psalm of David. The Lord is my shepherd, I shall not want,* they began to sing, as they dipped the bread in the brine. Old prayer books lay open, illuminated by the meager light of dusk. *He maketh me lie down in green pastures. He leadeth me beside the still waters.* They hummed and murmured.

"Reb Zev Wolf, sing *The Members of the Court*! Reb Zev Wolf! Reb Zev Wolf!" Jews would call out from every corner. "Sing *The Members of the Court* in the melody of Modcyz!" Every Sabbath Reb Zev would decline once. And then he would decline a second time. But the Jews knew that in the end Reb Zev Wolf would submit and sing *The Members of the Court* in the melody of Modcyz. Thus it was every Sabbath. Reb Zev was neither a cantor nor the son of a cantor, but at those third meals on Sabbath afternoon, in that quarter of Jerusalem, Reb Zev Wolf was a cantor. He and no one else. Reb Zev Wolf would close his eyes, one hand covering his ear, the other stroking his beard, as his voice picked up the melody…. While he chanted in the synagogue, his heart was elsewhere: in days long past and worlds far away, in the town of Modcyz. There, with his rebbe, when they sang *The Members of the Court* even the angels would come to listen to them. Here in the Zikhron Kedoshim synagogue there were no angels. Only a minyan of ten simple Jews, Jews of the Sabbath's third meal. *The members of the court.* Those Aramaic words, filled with mystery, absorbed the flavor of the Sabbath's third meal. Heads nodded, fingers tapped, eyes closed, Ephraim returned to Minsk, Abraham Isaac to Gur, Haim Mikhul to Warsaw. "To life! Jews, to life! Next year in Jerusalem." Abraham Isaac would rise from his seat and pour vodka into everyone's cups. All of a sudden there was movement around the table. Ephraim would stand up and shake the hand of every person in the group. After him, Haim Mikhul would do the same. And after him, they all did it. "To life, Abraham Isaac! To a good and peaceful life! To a complete recovery!" Abraham Isaac filled the cups once again, but his mind was in Gur. There in the *shteeble* in Gur, they had drunk vodka at the Sabbath's third meal. Where was that great congregation? Not a single one remained.

"Haim Mikhul, deliver a homily. Haim Mikhul, Haim Mikhul, deliver a homily." Every Sabbath, Haim Mikhul would decline once. And then he would decline a second time. But everyone knew that in the end Haim Mikhul would deliver a homily. Thus it was every Sabbath. Haim Mikhul was neither a rabbi nor the son of a rabbi, but at those third meals on Sabbath afternoon, in that quarter of Jerusalem, Haim Mikhul was the rabbi, he and no one else. "If it is written in this week's portion," Haim Mikhul would begin to intone in the lilt of a yeshiva student, "and Rashi says. What does Rashi say?" His mind was in the synagogue; his heart was in the *kloyz* in Warsaw. There, in the company of those who studied, they used to speak words of Torah. There, in the *kloyz* in Warsaw, they used to speak words of Torah. Haim Mikhul would finish speaking with *The Messiah, our righteous one, shall soon be revealed and bring us up to Jerusalem. Amen.*

"Well done, Haim Mikhul, well done," said the ashkenazim. But Ezra Siman Tov would call out, "Be strong and blessed."

The sun would have already set some time ago. Those waiting to recite the evening prayer would have already gathered in the synagogue and be chatting idly amongst themselves as they waited for those who were eating the third meal. They would look conspicuously at their watches and tap them with their fingers. "Ehh...nu...nu...." Those eating the third meal neither heard nor saw. They were not here, but in another world, in days long past and cities far away, in the houses of their fathers and the rabbis, in the *shteeble* and in the *kloyz*. They continued to sing the melody of their memories, in a tune filled with longing. *Soulmate, Father of Mercy, lead Thy servant to Thy will.* Neither the tune nor the accent was Ezra's. But the longing and the yearning were all his own. In this company Ezra Siman

Tov would eat the third meal. He could not understand every word they pronounced, nor did he recognize their melodies, but with his heart he felt he was one of them. As he was simple they were simple. It is fitting for the simple to dine with the simple.

Chapter four

In which we leave those eating the third meal at Zikhron Kedoshim to their memories, and recount what befell Ezra with the fiddler, Rahamim the Blind, at the *Tikkun Karet*.

Ezra pursued the mitzvot and courted them. He had never understood the remark of the Sages, that "the mitzvot were not prescribed for pleasure," and Rashi's gloss, "rather they were given as a burden upon your shoulders." Ezra truly derived great joy from performing the mitzvot. Taking the palm branch to recite hosannas, when the scent of citrons and myrtle filled the air of the synagogue; eating the unleavened bread on the night of Passover, when the house gleamed and the festive table was ringed by sons and daughters, sons-in-law and daughters-in-law; studying all through the night during the vigil of the festival of Shavuot or on the last night of the festival of Sukkot around a table laden with delicacies; these and the other mitzvot and holidays all brought him great happiness. For a long time before the holiday his heart would yearn for the moment when the mitzvah would be his to fulfill; for many days after the holiday he still derived great pleasure from it. When Haham Eliyahu Raful recited the story of Esther on Purim, Ezra's heart was as excited as if he were actually sitting in the palace of the king, waiting in trepidation to discover whether Ahasuerus would extend his golden scepter to Esther or if, heaven forefend, he would decree her death. When Haham Yosef Pinto chanted the book of Ruth in his distinctive voice, Ezra imagined himself walking in Bethlehem, gathering the ears of corn left behind by the farmers in the fields of Boaz, which overflowed with crops. He waited to see if Boaz would render himself vulnerable by taking Ruth as his wife or banish her from his presence instead. When they read in the weekly portion *And Judah came near to him, "For how shall I go up to my father, and the lad be not with me?"* his eyes brimmed with tears. Many remarkable tales had he heard from Haham Zion Ventura in the moments between the afternoon and evening prayers, but tales more pleasant than the story of Ruth the Moabite or Joseph and his brothers he had never heard. On the eve of the ninth day of Av, he sat low on the ground with the elders of the Zoharei Hamah Synagogue while Haham Eliyahu directed his mind and counted in his wailing voice the number of years since the destruction of the magnificent Temple and the exile of the holy nation from the sacred land. A lone candle illuminated the ark that had been stripped of its curtain, and a deep sigh tore his heart in two, *woe upon us, for we have sinned.* With his own eyes he could see the young priests throwing the keys of the shrine heavenwards and leaping into the flames that were devouring the Temple.

A radiant and happy countenance adorned Ezra's face throughout the entire year, except for the Days between the Straits and the Days of Penitence. From the seventeenth day of the month of Tammuz until the ninth day of Av a mournful gloom spread over Jerusalem and left a deep impression upon Ezra. During the Days of Penitence the tension and heaviness were apparent in his demeanor. From the day they announced the coming of the month of Elul in the Zoharei Hamah Synagogue up until the moment he emerged from the ritual bath on the eve of the Day of Atonement, a period of almost six weeks, a cloud hovered about him, as if he were a man anxious and concerned. In these weeks he increased his service of heaven and spent less time on idle matters, rising early to recite the penitential prayers and remaining silent for long stretches of time, augmenting his almsgiving and beneficence to acquire advocates in the heavenly court. During this period, Haham Menashe would rid his homilies of humorous and entertaining tales and deliver words of chastisement and ethical rebuke, filling his sermons with discussions of *Sha'are Teshuvah* by Rabbenu Jonah the Pietist or *The Duties of the Heart* by Rabbenu Bahya. Ezra Siman Tov would listen to the penitential prayers and hymns and shake with anticipation. Their words would take hold of his heart:

> *My youthful vigor cares but for itself. When will I my*
> *haughty spirit save?*
> *And how may I my maker truly serve, when I am but my*
> *carnal passion's slave?*
> *What can I utter? Implacable desires pursue me from child-*
> *hood to the grave.*

His heart shuddered at the gravity of judgment. The verses repeated themselves in his mind throughout the day and would not relent for even the slightest moment:

> *My youthful vigor cares but for itself. When will I my*
> *haughty spirit save?*
> *My youthful vigor cares but for itself. When will I my*
> *haughty spirit save?*

He was filled with terror of the Day of Judgment. Each time he arrived at the appeal for repentance in the prayer of the eighteen blessings, his eyes filled with tears and the memory of the folly committed in his youth loomed before him and did not leave him. Hard and painful the deed had been, and still more painful was its memory. At those moments the sigh of the poet would appear before him:

Whither may I turn for succor, for support on judgment day?
Constantly my sins surround me; I flush with shame, in disarray;
If my friends could scent my errors, they would flee without delay.

For several years he wept and pleaded for his sin to be pardoned, and he scrubbed and scoured the stain with all his might. But every year during the penitential days it seemed to him as though his sin returned and stood mockingly before him: "You think that you have erased the stain. You err." And he could tell that his sin spoke truthfully. Ezra well knew what the Torah promised about repentance, that the sages had said, "Great is repentance for it reaches unto the Throne of Glory," but "*the heart recognizes its own bitterness.*" But he felt the impure thoughts about that sin accompany him, for they had not been entirely uprooted and they filled him with shame. On one occasion a man celebrated for his righteousness arrived in the city, and all Ezra's friends paid a visit to him to request prayers for the sick, advice about matchmaking, counsel for a profitable livelihood, guidance for salvation, or to receive his special blessing for success. But Ezra, who was not in the habit of doing such things, refrained from going to the righteous man for such matters. It occurred to him rather that he should pay him a visit to ask if the signs of his sin were still visible on his face, for he had once heard from Haham Pinto that the truly righteous can discern a sin by looking at a person's face or examining a specimen of his handwriting. He waited a long time until his turn arrived, but as soon as he reached the doorway he retreated. He said to himself, "In truth, the matter depends only upon me. How will the words of the righteous man be of any benefit to me? If I am worthy and my resources are adequate to repair my sin, the Torah has already promised me *And unto thee shall be his desire, and thou shalt rule over him.* When I have attained such merit, I shall sense within myself that I have been victorious. Yet if the impression of the sin remains etched in my heart, I must not have cleansed myself of it, and how will righteous men help me when the matter depends upon me alone?"

Thus he walked, meditating upon repentance and filled with shame, throughout the time between the first days of the month of Elul and the eve of the Day of Atonement. On the eve of the Day of Atonement, after having been flogged on his back with a calf-skin strap by the beadle of the synagogue, Benjamin Assoulin, in commemoration of the forty lashes; after his lips had uttered the verse three times, *But He, being full of compassion, forgave their iniquity, and destroyed them not: yea, many a time He turned his anger away, and did not stir up all His wrath;* after he had descended and immersed himself in the pure waters of the ritual bath in order to fulfill what is said, that *we have come through fire and water,* and had emerged and dried off; only then, at that moment, was it apparent that his sin had been reconciled. A certain spirit of purity and appeasement spread throughout the world. At that instant, even the slightest memory of the sin seemed fleeting, and he was filled with love toward the entire world. When he sat in the Zoharei Hamah synagogue before the opening prayer, *Kol Nidre,* with the entire congregation wrapped in white prayer shawls, and listened to Haham Eliyahu Raful begin the hymn *To Thee my God, my yearning. In Thee, my soul and my mind, my breath and my spirit,* he felt his heart fill with great longing and tenderness. When Haham Raful reached the closing lines of the hymn:

> *With my whole heart, Thee have I sought;*
> *May my request not be for naught.*
> *Wash out my errors in thy grace,*
> *With tears I shed before thy face;*
> *Truly my soul has said its piece*
> *Through Thee my God I seek my peace*
> *Gather in with love my sin*
> *On the day that I am gathered in,*
> *The day when I to meet Thee go*
> *Accept my Lord my conduct so*
> *And grant to me my just reward*

For those that follow Thee, O Lord.

Send to me thy angels of grace,
Let them quickly towards me race.
With one accord would they welcome me
And greet me as I come to Thee.
Before Thee may the light concealed
Serve as my buckler and my shield;
Beneath the shelter of thy wing
May I forever to thee cling.

His entire being shook and stirred as if a spirit of purity from the recesses of the synagogue had settled upon him. Once, in those very moments, a thought had occurred to him: Would that when the time comes for me to depart from the world I might depart with that very hymn and melody.

Every Thursday night a group of several members of the congregation, roughly twice the size of a minyan, assembled in the Zoharei Hamah Synagogue to hold a *Tikkun Karet*, a ceremony for spiritual restoration. They would arrive two hours before midnight and study a particular set of teachings with Haham Menashe Levi and with the aged mystic Haham Yosef Salem. At midnight they would recite the *Tikkun Hatzot*, *Tikkun Rachel*, *Tikkun Leah*, and *Redemption of Souls* for those dangerously ill, and then would continue to study throughout the night until sunrise. They worshipped at dawn like the men of olden times and then retired to their homes. This was called the *tikkun karet* because it saved a man from punishment for the gravest category of sins; those that the Torah decrees worthy of death at the hands of heaven. It was also said that this study had a particular benefit—that the pain brought to the eyes by the night protected a man from sinning with his eyes during the day. In Jerusalem they used to say in hushed tones that Haham Yosef's revered father had been worthy to receive the holy spirit. When Ezra Siman Tov was a child, he had accompanied his father to the afternoon prayer at the synagogue of the mystics, Beit El. The mystics performed the afternoon prayer wearing great tefillin. They stood in silence with their thick prayer books, which contained specific instructions on how to direct the mind during prayer, and the synagogue filled with the fear of God. Once Ezra saw the Haham's prayer shawl on fire and hastily pulled at his father's coat, calling in alarm: "Father, the Haham's prayer shawl is on fire!" One of the mystics heard him and turned to him, saying "Fear not, it is not on fire. Keep silent!" he added, "Do not tell the entire world what you have just witnessed."

Every week Ezra scrupulously participated in the ceremony, but he only arrived after they recited the *Tikkun Hatzot*. No one ever asked him why. This was the custom of the Jerusalem faithful: they never asked unnecessary questions. But where was Ezra during those hours when his friends were already participating in the *Tikkun Karet*? At that time he would walk through Nahlaot, down a small alleyway off Betzalel Street next to the synagogue of the Jarmulkim, and then descend ten steps to arrive at the house of the celebrated musician, Rahamim Kalifa.

Rahamim was a great artist. He was also blind. A lonely, childless man. An extraordinary player of the 'oud, kanun, and violin. The most celebrated cantors of Jerusalem would come to him to learn the transitions between musical scales and the melodies of the ancient hymns. For several years he had hardly set foot outside his own home. In moments of inspiration he would sit next to the window with the kanun and hum a new melody that no one had ever heard before. The cantors who sat with him would strain their ears attempting to capture the melody, and use it on the Sabbath in the synagogues of Jerusalem in Mahane Yehudah or the Bukharan Quarter when reciting *Nishmat Kol Hai*, the kaddish, or the prayer of sanctification. The cantors had learned many melodies from Rahamim, each one different from the others. What they all had in common was the pain that pulsed through them and melted the hardness of every heart. Yet they were not entirely forlorn—a thin thread of light always sprang forth full of hope, and even the pain itself was gentle. Those who came to worship never knew where the cantors had learned their new melodies, and the cantors never troubled to tell them. Rahamim knew that the cantors took his melodies and sang them, but did not protest. On the contrary, his heart filled with joy, knowing that it was through his melodies that the Children of Israel purified themselves before their Maker and sanctified Him. Only once did Rahamim assert his right, when a young cantor took a large number of his melodies, altered them slightly, and preened about them as if they were his own. Rahamim did not utter a word, but whenever that cantor entered his home, he would immediately sense his presence, cease singing and playing, and remain silent. The cantor pleaded with him to sing, but was unsuccessful. Rahamim never once told him his reason.

Ezra Siman Tov would come to Rahamim's house every Thursday evening armed with two overflowing baskets. Tiptoeing silently, he opened the door quietly. As soon as Ezra put his hand on the doorknob, Rahamim would recognize him and call out "Ezra, welcome." Ezra did not go to learn melodies, for Ezra was neither a cantor nor a musician, but as soon as he arrived, he picked up a broom and swept the house free of dust, filled a bucket with water and washed the floor. Afterwards, he would take a rag and wipe the dust off the few pieces of furniture in the room. In the kitchen he would wash the dishes that lay in the sink, then put a pot of water on to boil and put away the food he had brought with him for the Sabbath. He would prepare a mug of hot tea, bring it to Rahamim and sit down at his side. Every Thursday Rahamim asked Ezra to tell him a story, and Ezra would do so. When Ezra finished telling his tale, Rahamim would pick up his violin, tuck it under his chin, pick up his bow, focus his thoughts as if he were standing at prayer, and fill the room with sweet and pleasing sounds. Throughout the week he played the kanun; this was the only time that he touched his aged fiddle. Every week he played the same melody on his violin, except each time it seemed as if it were a different one, as he would emphasize a passage that suited the story Ezra was telling on that occasion, taking part in the unfolding of the narrative. The violin sighed, wept softly, cried; then it moaned, wavered, and prayed; then it opened a window onto a new world and seemed to laugh as if it were floating and dancing lightly. Ezra closed his eyes in those moments as if his spirit had left his body and floated through other worlds.

At last Rahamim would put down his bow, raise his chin from the violin, stroke Ezra's hand and ask, "Did you understand?" Ezra never responded. Once Rahamim asked him, "Ezra, what would you call the story told by my violin?" Ezra was silent. Rahamim turned to him. "If I were to take a title from Scripture, I would call it *My soul, wait thou only upon God; for my expectation is from Him;* from the writings of the sages, I would call it *The Lord Desires Thy Heart.*" Ezra remained silent. When he got up to leave, a phrase from one of the dawn hymns occurred to him and stood in front of him, pleading. He said to Rahamim, "I would call it, *The Dawning of the Day.*"

That night, Ezra Siman Tov left him in peace and went to the Zoharei Hamah Synagogue as usual. In his whole life, Ezra had never heard such a melody, or anything like it; and Rahamim had never performed such a melody, not on any other day, or for anyone else. Neither Rahamim nor Ezra ever told anyone about this melody. It was a secret between the two of them. Who knew its meaning?

One time, the great brother-in-law, Doctor Yehudah Tawil, met Ezra Siman Tov as he was walking out of Rahamim's house. Doctor Tawil was walking back to Rehavia on his way home from a reception held by scholarly friends in honor of one of their colleagues, who had received an honorary degree at the university in Jerusalem. His great book on Ibn Gabirol tucked beneath his arm, he was smiling at the new insight he had discovered in interpreting one of Ibn Gabirol's most difficult hymns and delighting in the praise he had received from his fellow scholars. Ezra walked down Betzalel Street towards him, a man preoccupied with his affairs, amazed by the melody of the violin. Doctor Tawil said to him, "Ezra, are you not one of the stalwarts of Zoharei Hamah? Is it not Thursday night tonight? Everyone thinks that you are performing the *Tikkun Karet*. What are you doing here?" He laughed and continued, "Ezra, perhaps you have already performed all of your ceremonies?"

Ezra was stunned for a moment. He lowered his eyes to the

ground and responded, "Yes, this was my *Tikkun Karet*," and then fell silent.

Chapter five

In which we leave Doctor Tawil laughing and Ezra silent on Betzalel Street, and recount the astounding tale Ezra Siman Tov heard from Haham Ventura.

If you were to think Ezra had only good days you would be greatly mistaken. Is there anyone who has only good days? Most days a person spends surrounded by troubles and pains, burden after burden heaping upon his shoulders, tiring him out and offering no respite, and some weigh upon him so greatly that were the Holy One, Blessed be He, not his helper, he could not bear them. Great troubles have not passed Ezra Siman Tov by, and although in all of his days we have only seen him enjoying good fortune, and never heard a complaint or even a sigh escape his lips, all this is only because he has accustomed his tongue to say "This too is for the best." For thus we have been taught, "a man must bless the bad as well as the good," for the psalmist says, *I will take the cup of salvation and call upon the name the Lord.* Elsewhere he says, *Though I find anguish and sorrow I call upon the name of the Lord.* Ezra applied to himself the words of David, *I will sing of mercy and judgment*, interpreting them thus: if I encounter mercy, I sing; but if I encounter judgment I also sing. Ezra had not only trained his tongue to do this, he had even trained his mind to do so. He was grateful for the good moments as if they were a generous favor, not his just deserts. As another psalm says, *Who remembered us in our low estate, his mercy endureth forever.*

He had no demands upon the world. He had once heard Haham Pinto explain the following passage of the Talmud in Tractate Berachot: Hillel the elder was once on the road and heard the sound of crying from the city. He said to himself, I am sure that this cry did not come from my own home. But, asked Haham Pinto, how was Hillel so confident this cry had not come from his own home? Is anyone so sure that his house is immune from trouble? No, rather, Haham Yosef explained, Hillel was confident that if the cry had come from the city, it had not come from his own home, for the members of his household did not cry out, even when they had great troubles. Once Ezra heard Haham Zion Ventura tell a tale about the righteous brothers, Rabbi Elimelech of Lyzhansk and Rabbi Zusha. The learned Rabbi Zusha experienced terrible troubles his entire life, with no respite. Once a man who had endured a great misfortune went to Rabbi Elimelech. He said, "Rabbi, I have come to ask a question."

"Ask, my son," he replied.

"The sages said a man must bless the bad the same way he blesses the good, but does this mean we must accept our sorrows with joy? Rabbi," said the man to Rabbi Elimelech, "please, I entreat you to explain this saying to me, for my mind cannot bear it."

Rabbi Elimelech responded, "My son, you have asked a profound question, for this saying is a difficult one, and I cannot explain it to you, but hasten to my brother, Rabbi Zusha, and he will explain it to you."

The man set out on a long journey through forests and fields. Terribly fatigued, he finally found Rabbi Zusha, who was caught between two fires and afflicted by great torment. He said to him, "Rabbi, your brother, Rabbi Elimelech, sent me to ask you to explain the saying of the rabbis, that a man must accept afflictions with happiness."

Rabbi Zusha was amazed and said to him, "It is odd that my brother sent you to me to explain this statement. How can I explain this to you when I have never experienced afflictions?"

On only one occasion did Ezra nearly cry out. When his own house experienced that same distress that shook the entire city of Jerusalem, then Ezra wept and cried out in a voice that made hearts tremble, "My Lord, My Lord, why have you deserted me?" But he quickly mastered himself and stopped protesting against Heaven. When he read the verses in the book of Psalms that described something like that which had occurred, he would read them in a weeping voice, without a tune, as if he were thinking about himself and the Master of the World. But he would then immediately say to himself, the true Judge, His judgments are just and true. Measure for measure. My sins brought this about. May it be His will that my afflictions serve as an altar of expiation.

When he went to comfort people in mourning he recounted, almost incidentally, how he too had been afflicted, for one who experiences great misfortune, may such a thing never happen to us or you, believes that all misfortune has only befallen him, and no suffering in the entire world is like his. When he hears of someone whose misfortunes are greater he takes comfort. Such is the way of the world. The mourners listened to his misfortune and took comfort. Once one of the good men of Jerusalem lost his beloved son, a handsome young man, to enemy fire in one of Israel's wars. All the Jerusalem faithful went to comfort him, but he could not accept their consolation, and out of deep anguish he began to lose his mind and go blind. They told Ezra Siman Tov. Ezra Siman Tov went to the great and eminent rabbi who headed the academy in Rehavia, a man whose mind was so sharp that the sages of Israel were terrified of his countenance but whose heart was as soft as that of a pure boy, filled with love for all. The Gaon, the eminent scholar, was immersed in the preparation of an extremely erudite lesson on the tractate Bava Kama. All the students knew that when he prepared a theoretical lesson no one was allowed to speak with him; if someone were to enter his presence, the rabbi would not even notice him. But when Ezra Siman Tov entered the rabbi's presence, the rabbi raised his eyes from the volume of the Talmud that lay before him, listened to what Ezra said, closed the book, put on his coat and said to him, "Come with me and we shall go to him." They went to him.

The Gaon entered and sat down. He put his head between his hands, saying nothing. The mourner sitting opposite him was silent as well. Out of respect for the Gaon a hush fell over all the visitors and a heavy silence filled the room. The rabbi began to speak and said: "Divine justice is difficult." He repeated, "Divine justice is difficult. Many years have passed, half a jubilee. I stood in a forest outside of Vilna. There were tall trees on either side. A faint glimmer of sunshine flickered through the thick branches. I was fleeing, gathering berries and herbs in the forest, and my beloved son was on my right. He was a wunderkind, all had predicted great things for him. All of a sudden an evil officer stood before me, a pistol in his hand and a sneer on his lips. He raised his pistol and fired. And my son fell before my very eyes. The officer allowed me to live only to increase my torment. At that moment the words of Scripture suddenly appeared before me, *The precious sons of Zion, comparable to fine gold, how are they esteemed as earthen pitchers, the work of the hands of the potter!* We were refugees in a forest. In a foreign land. No one to take pity, no one to have mercy. Your son was a soldier in a Jewish state and fell in its defense." The mourner's eyes brimmed with tears and he nodded his head.

And so Ezra conducted himself throughout his days. Those bearing afflictions or enduring illnesses would often come to him to complain and recount their sufferings, for such is the way of the world, people love to recount their afflictions and their complaints to their friends, but if their friends respond and recount their own misfortunes they leave them and go to others. For a person never likes to hear about his friend's misfortunes, are his own misfortunes not enough that he should add to them those of his friend? So those bearing afflictions went to Ezra, who listened patiently and never complained, and they left comforted.

One day Ezra left the synagogue after hearing Haham Ventura's memorial address to mark the one-year anniversary of the death of a particular judge. He saw the writer waiting for him at the entrance to the synagogue. Immediately he said to him, "Sir, you have come at a good time. Listen to the tale recounted today by Haham Ventura. It is a tale that Rabbi Haim Yosef David Azulai wrote about the eminent religious judge, Haham Haim Kafusi of Cairo, the author of a commentary on two ancient works of midrash, whose eyes grew dim until he was beset by blindness and could no longer see. When he heard the people murmuring that he had lost his vision because he had taken bribes, he assembled the entire congregation in the synagogue, mounted the dais and said, 'I have heard such-and-such slander, and because of these rumors, this terrible desecration of God's name, behold I pray before God, if their slander is true, let me stay like this, but if they are circulating lies, may God light up my eyes and let them see as they once did.' His eyes were immediately opened and he began to look upon each member of the congregation and call upon each individual by name; suddenly they were terrified of his countenance. From that day on, he affixed a phrase to all his signatures on his legal decisions: 'The Lord is my banner, Haim Kafusi.' Rabbi Azulai wrote that he had seen his signature before the event and it was illegible; but after the miracle it was clear and bold."

The writer chuckled and said to him, "Does this tale stand on its own or is it a new chapter in your tale?"

Ezra responded, "What do I know? I heard a tale from Haham Ventura, and I recounted it to you. But you are the writer and you know how tales unfold." The writer was silent, and Ezra was silent.

Chapter six

In which we leave the writer chuckling, standing silently in his place and recount what happened to Ezra with Reb Moishe Dovid and the Rabbenu Tam tefillin.

Every Sabbath, Ezra diligently went to hear the Haham's sermon after the early-afternoon service. The Haham was Haham Yosef Pinto, one of the humble sages of Jerusalem, a scholar who had not a single stain upon his character. The residents of Jerusalem who used to hear the sermons of Haham Yosef on the Sabbath tasted in them all the possible flavors of the world, everyone who listened savored whichever flavor he sought. Little children enjoyed the charm of the pleasant stories; youths appreciated the acrostics and numerology; ordinary people, the scriptural commentary; scholars, the reasoning behind the laws; pietists, pious teachings that enabled a man to cling to his Father in heaven; elders, ethical rebuke that shattered the hearts of men; and everyone took away a bit of comfort from words on the salvation that would soon come to Israel. Although we have said that his sermons contained all the flavors of the world, in truth there were several missing: those of dispute and quarrel, of slander or humiliation of the sages. Those who could not appreciate a sermon if it lacked at least the slightest insinuation of these attitudes did not go to the sermons of Haham Pinto. Ezra Siman Tov held dear all the meanings of his sermons. After each sermon he used what he had heard to examine himself and ascertain how he could improve his observance of the law or his practice of ethics. Thus he had once heard from Haham Pinto, in the name of the great rabbi, the author of *The Pele Yo'etz*: each time a person has learned something he should apply the appropriate lesson to himself.

On each and every Sabbath Haham Pinto based his sermon upon one of the mitzvot mentioned in the weekly portion. One Sabbath he expounded upon the mitzvah concerning the tefillin. He opened with a discussion of their holiness, which indeed is very great and serves as an ornament to Israel: for the entire time that a member of the house of Israel sits crowned with the tefillin, he bears witness to the unity of God's name. Humility settles upon him and grace extends over him. He avoids silliness and frivolity. Scripture says, *The Lord hath sworn by his right hand, and by the arm of his strength*, and the Talmud comments, "even God Himself puts on tefillin." Haham Pinto interpreted these lines thus: *His right hand* this is the Torah; *the arm of his strength*, these are the tefillin. Much the same way we profess the unity of God by repeating, *Hear O Israel, the Lord our God, The Lord is one*, God himself unifies us, as Scripture says: *And what one nation in the earth is like Thy people, even like Israel*. Although His love has not yet been revealed, and the entire world does not acknowledge it, this is only because the tefillin that wrap a man's arm are customarily covered. In the future they will be uncovered, and everyone will see His love. Concerning those days, the prophet says, *The Lord hath made bare His holy arm in the eyes of all the nations; and all the ends of the earth shall see the salvation of our God*.

Ezra listened carefully to all the Haham said. He, who cherished all of the mitzvot, treasured the mitzvah of the tefillin more than any other, constantly stroking the straps to prevent his mind from wandering and even kissing them affectionately from time to, time. When he put them on, he secured the tefillin on his hand in *an expanded place that heals the hand* as Scripture says, opposite his heart, ensuring the knot remained secure; the tefillin on his head rested precisely on the spot where a baby's head is particularly soft, and he ensured that their leather straps did not turn over, for he had once heard from Haham Pinto that when a single leather strap of Rav Huna's tefillin turned over, he fasted for forty days. In short, he treated them with great respect. Only after he had read the daily selection of Bible, Talmud and *Zohar* from the *Hok L'Yisrael* would he take off his tefillin, removing them slowly and folding them as if they were the wings of a dove, for he had heard from Haham Yosef Pinto about Elisha, the man of wings, who, while wearing tefillin in a time of persecution, was stopped by a Roman captain, and hid his tefillin in his hand.

The captain asked him, "What do you have there in your hands?"

"The wings of a dove," he replied. He opened his hand and there were the wings of a dove. Why specifically the wings of a dove? For Israel is likened to them, as Scripture says *as the wings of a dove covered with silver.* After having folded them up like the wings of a dove, he placed them in a light-blue velvet satchel sewn especially for him by his wife Madame Sarah, embroidered with silver thread, stitched with the love of a wife for her husband, and she had written his initials: E.S.T, Ezra Siman Tov, which could also be read as Ezra Sephardi Tahor, Ezra, a pure Sephardi; as well as the letters S and G—Servant of God.

Ezra Siman Tov had once heard a lesson from the *Book of Trembling*, that every man in the house of Israel should take upon himself one mitzvah that will be particularly special to him, and which he will exalt more than any other, and that mitzvah will accompany him. The Haham likened it to a man who is drowning at sea but grabs on to one branch with all of his might and is saved. Immediately after hearing this, Ezra said to himself that he would grasp onto the tefillin. As he was speaking, Haham Pinto had recounted Rabbenu Tam's argument with his grandfather, Rashi, about the order of the passages in the boxes of the tefillin. Because of that dispute, those who fear heaven, the pietists and the mystics, don two pairs of tefillin every day, one with Rashi's preferred order and the other with that of Rabbenu Tam, to fulfill the mitzvah according to both opinions.

When Ezra heard these words from the mouth of the Haham, he was greatly startled. He had never heard that Rabbenu Tam was the grandson of Rashi or that there were two different types of tefillin. If the opinion of Rabbenu Tam were revealed as true, then he would never have put on legitimate tefillin in his life. If this were so, then he was like the irreligious, heaven forbid, like the heads that had never worn tefillin. Without delay he decided to don the Rabbenu Tam tefillin as well.

Immediately after reciting the blessing to mark the conclusion of the Sabbath, Ezra Siman Tov would do something filled with holiness, to ensure the coming week was successful. The week after the tefillin sermon, Ezra Siman Tov walked to Malakhi Street in Ge'ulah, to Haham Mas'oud Baghdadi, a professional scribe. Haham Baghdadi, celebrated throughout Jerusalem for the beauty and holiness of his writing, used to immerse himself in the ritual bath each time he wrote out the name of God, and the pietists of Jerusalem as well as her sages wore the tefillin he wrote. Ezra asked him to compose a set of Rabbenu Tam tefillin for him. Haham Mas'oud was surprised. Who was this man before him? Ezra, whom he had known for many years, had ordered tefillin for all of his sons, and every year during the month of Elul would bring the mezuzahs from his home for inspection. He used to give his prayer shawl to Ezra for cleaning and pressing before the New Year; he had never sent his prayer shawl to be cleaned by anyone besides Ezra Siman Tov. When his prayer shawl was sent back and he wrapped himself in it on the New Year, Haham Mas'oud used to say to the members of his household that he felt a certain brightness in it, for the craftsman who performs his craft with purpose and sincerity makes his work shine before him. Haham Zion Ventura had once recounted a story about a spiritual leader whose followers had ordered a bed for him from a worthy craftsman. After several days, they saw that he was not sleeping upon it. When they asked him why the bed had not found favor in his eyes, if it had not been made properly or the craftsman who made it was unworthy, he said to them, "It is a good bed and a worthy man has made it, but what can I do? Since you brought it to me, I cannot sleep, for as soon as I lie upon it, the memory of the destruction of our holy Temple appears before me and my eyes brim with tears of anguish." They went out and discovered that the craftsman, a God-fearing man, had made the bed during the Days between the Straits. As he made it, he had sighed for the destruction of the Temple and his eyes had brimmed with tears.

Haham Mas'oud was surprised. Why did Ezra want Rabbenu Tam tefillin? Ezra was a simple man, not a pietist. But one who sees many things in the world wonders less and less. Haham Mas'oud Baghdadi had seen much throughout his life in Jerusalem, and more than he had seen, he had heard, like the story about the cobbler who used to sit on HaNevi'im Street and repair shoes; no one knew anything about him, but when he died and the great men of Jerusalem followed his bier, it became known that he was one of the hidden righteous, and that several severe decrees of heaven had been annulled because of his merit. Or the story about the elderly porter on Porters' Street at the corner of Jaffa Road, whose back was always laden with heavy bags and parcels, about whom the pietists of Jerusalem used to whisper that his merit protected half of the city. So Haham Mas'oud did not ask or even utter a word. Who knew? He fixed a date for Ezra, took his deposit and said goodbye.

One day, Haham Mas'oud sent for Ezra to notify him that the Rabbenu Tam tefillin he had ordered were waiting for him. The day that the Rabbenu Tam tefillin were delivered to Ezra Siman Tov was like a festival for him. Madame Sarah had sewn a white velvet satchel for him and embroidered the initials of Rabbenu Tam on the cover, to prevent confusion with the Rashi tefillin. From the moment he received the tefillin, his heart yearned to wear them. The next day, after the public repetition of the morning prayer and the recitation of the psalm *Happy are they that dwell in Thy house*, Ezra removed the Rashi tefillin, kissed them affectionately, and as if seeking their pardon, said to them, "You will not be insulted if I remove you in order to put on the Rabbenu Tam tefillin, for he was your beloved grandson, and I once heard from Haham Pinto, 'a man is jealous of everyone except for his sons and his students. Why is he not jealous of them? For he says to himself, "they are my own, and have taken from me what they can," and most certainly there is peace in heaven between Rashi and his grandson Rabbenu Tam.'"

At that very moment, the visage of his own beloved grandson appeared before him. How much did he delight in playing with him! He was his first grandson. He would sit on Ezra's lap, hang on his neck, and roll about calling, "Grandpa, Grandpa." Only yesterday he had started Talmud Torah, accompanied by both Ezra and Madame Sarah on his walk from the house. They had covered his head with a prayer shawl to prevent him from seeing forbidden images before he saw the letters of the sacred language. His grandmother, Madame Sarah, whispered prayers for his protection as tears welled up in the corner of her eyes, and she wrapped a scarf around the boy's neck to prevent harm, heaven forbid, from the morning chill of Jerusalem. In order to render the words of the Torah sweet to him, she gave him sesame candies dipped in honey and colorful squares of Turkish delight with pistachios, for sweet things accustom the tongue to words of Torah.

When they had arrived at the teacher's, Ezra laid his hands upon his grandson's head and recited a blessing: "May he be worthy to study the Torah for its own sake and with love," and prayed on his behalf, that "he grow in his knowledge of the Torah."

They say the child has a sharp mind. Perhaps, who knows, Ezra thought, I will merit that one of my offspring becomes a scholar, one whose craft is the Torah and who studies the most difficult passages in the Talmud. How much did he yearn for this! Ezra held the sages in great esteem. Each time he caught sight of young yeshiva students poring over the great folio volumes of the Talmud, he looked at them with adulation, for the study of Torah was their craft, and they labored to the point of exhaustion in their trade. He would say to himself, "Not everyone is worthy, I was not, perhaps my son's son will be." Each and every day, after the young yeshiva students had finished studying and left the books they had used in a disordered pile on the table, Ezra would hold each book in his hands with affection, straighten out the creases they had left on the pages and return them to their proper place on the shelf.

In the midst of these reflections, Ezra took out the Rabbenu Tam tefillin from their satchel and his heart filled with joy as he prepared to wear them. With four fingers of his right hand he covered his eyes and recited the *Shema*, lengthening the final word of the first verse, *One*, and meditating in his prayers on the unity of the Creator, a singularity without parallel, who reigns over the seven firmaments, the earth, and the four winds of heaven. When he began the next paragraph and uttered the words, *And thou shall love the Lord, thy God*, he intended to love God with his entire heart, more than he loved others; at the words *with all thy soul*, he intended to offer his life for the sake of God's unity. He imagined himself before a great blazing fire, tormentors asking him, "Either renounce your faith and receive all the good of the world or you will be thrown into this fire," and responding, *Hear O Israel, the Lord our God, the Lord is one*.

As he did this, an *avrech** was staring at him. At first, Ezra did not notice, for he felt happy that he was worthy to put on tefillin according to the law, and one who feels such happiness sees only the good that surrounds him, but after having put them on and reciting *Hear O Israel*, as well as *Happy are they that dwell in Thy house* and *The redeemer shall come to Zion and unto them that turn from transgression*, he noticed that the man was continuing to stare at him and detected a measure of rebuke in his gaze. Ezra could not understand what he had done for this man to look at him with such reproach. He thought that perhaps he had not put on his tefillin in their proper place and began to adjust them to ensure they lay on his head squarely between his eyes. As he was doing so, the *avrech* approached him. He said to him, "Ezra, I know that you are an honest man, but why have you taken off the Rashi tefillin and put on the Rabbenu Tam tefillin? You have acted improperly!"

---

* a term used to describe somebody who learns Torah full-time.

Astonished, Ezra replied, "This is what I heard in the Haham's sermon this past Sabbath."

The man responded severely, "I have no idea which Haham delivered the sermon, nor do I know what he said, but know that you have acted improperly and one does not derive the law from storytellers. If you studied something once, you did not repeat it; if you repeated it, you repeated it only once; if you repeated it several times, it was not properly explained to you, for the explanation of the Torah is not entrusted to the common people but to the sages. The mitzvot of the Torah were not given for a person's pleasure, to find peace and quiet for his soul; rather they were given as a yoke upon the neck of Israel, who must fulfill them according to the letter of the law, as a slave before a king. Know that according to the law, a simple man is not worthy to put on Rabbenu Tam tefillin, only a man who has repaired the sins of his youth and is celebrated for his piety can wear them." The *avrech* finished what he was saying and went on his way. That *avrech* was Reb Moishe Dovid.

Ezra did not know what to do. The words of the *avrech* pierced his heart. He felt perplexed. With his entire being he had wanted to wear Rabbenu Tam tefillin, he had even taken upon himself an irrevocable vow, but how could he possibly say about himself that he was celebrated for his piety? He was a simple man, with simple habits. He began to think. He examined each and every one of his deeds, from the moment he arose from sleep and expressed gratitude for his pure soul until he lay down on his bed, repented for the misdeeds of that day and entrusted his soul to his Creator, but did not find a single deed over the course of his entire day that he could call an act of piety. He prayed at dawn with proper intentions like the other members of the Zoharei Hamah Synagogue; observed fixed times for the study of Torah and read the *Hok L'Yisrael* at the conclusion of the service as did most members of that congregation; went to his work and conducted his business in good faith; supported his family honorably as was the way of the world; loved his wife as if they were one flesh; honored her even more than he honored himself, as the sages had instructed; enjoyed the mitzvot and observed them meticulously like all legitimate members of the house of Israel; avoided slander; never mistreated his fellow man; gave as much charity as he could afford; soothed the downtrodden with words of comfort; rejoiced and brought joy to others at the bridal canopy of an orphaned bride; extended true kindness by caring for the dead; attended the sermons of the Haham on the Sabbath; yearned constantly for Israel's redemption; and so he conducted himself, but every member of the house of Israel conducts himself thus, how could he think of himself as celebrated for his piety? And what is more, every day he tried to repent. Who could possibly know the bitterness of his soul about the misdeed of his youth, which stood before him and would not move? Who knew when he would be worthy to repair it?

On weekdays when Ezra had a rabbinic question he used to ask Haham Menashe Kahanof after the afternoon prayers and his class on *The Ben Ish Hai*; on the Sabbath he would ask Haham Yosef Pinto after his sermon. The day of Reb Moishe Dovid's rebuke, he approached Haham Menashe. He said to him, "Rabbi, I have a question to ask."

The Haham replied, "Ask, my son."

Ezra told him the entire incident of the Rabbenu Tam tefillin.

"Continue as you are doing," the Haham brusquely responded. To himself, however, he murmured, "*The innocence of the upright will guide them.*" The Haham did not explain his decision, nor did he instruct Ezra on how to respond to the *avrech*, but Ezra did not seek an explanation. Such was his way whenever he posed a question to the Haham. Ezra followed Haham Menashe's ruling and continued to put on Rabbenu Tam tefillin, but the sweet enjoyment that he had experienced the first time he put them on grew faint. Pain is forgotten with the passing of time, such is the way of the world. But it leaves an impression where it first appeared. This impression of pain was stamped in Ezra's heart, as he continued on his way.

Chapter seven

In which we leave aside the feelings etched on Ezra's heart, and recount what befell him with the youth in the tattered *kapota*.

One night after the evening prayer in the Zoharei Hamah Synagogue a youth approached Ezra. His face looked like that of a Jerusalem Sephardi but his dress was that of the Ashkenazi Hasidim: thin sidelocks, a tattered *kapota*, and dark sad eyes. Ezra turned toward him to see if he was seeking charity for a poor bride or someone ill and reached for his wallet, but the youth said to him, "I am not seeking charity, but a favor."

"What sort of favor?" asked Ezra.

"I am requesting," said the youth, "I am requesting that you come with me to take a short walk in the woods. It is wonderful to walk among the trees in the evening. To hear their voices. To listen to the singing of the grass. We are accustomed to go once a month to pour out our hearts and be alone among the trees in order to attain spiritual union through happiness, but we only go in the company of another, so as not reach a state of prohibited isolation. Tonight, however, I have no one to accompany me. I beseech you, come with me. I will not prolong it unduly nor will I trouble you greatly, and what is more, with the help of the blessed Creator, together we shall merit the fulfillment of spiritual union in happiness. Together and together through happiness!"

Ezra observed him, saw the expression of great pain on his face, and wanted to do him a favor, but this evening stroll through a forest in the middle of the week, he could not understand it, it was not familiar to him. Occasionally the youth of Jerusalem would go hiking in large groups on the middle days of a festival or on *Lag Ba'Omer* and have a picnic at Shimon HaTzaddik or on the hill near the landmark of Samuel the Prophet that the Arabs call *Nebi Samwil*, but he knew nothing about the spiritual union spoken of by the Hasid. Ezra said to him, "my family is waiting for me to come home, and I am concerned that they may worry, but since you are requesting a favor, I shall go and accompany you."

Together they walked along the path, while the youth explained to Ezra that one could only serve God through enormous happiness and complete faith, adducing proofs from Scripture, sayings of the sages and statements from his own rabbi. As he was walking, he periodically emitted sighs heavy enough to shatter his entire body. They arrived at the valley below the shantytown at the end of Betzalel Street. Darkness covered the valley, and it was deserted except for scattered olive trees and thorn bushes. The Hasid stopped next to one of the olive trees, took a small bottle of water from the pocket of his *kapota*, washed his hands, tied his prayer belt and readied himself for prayer. In his entire life Ezra had never seen prayer like this. The youth was speaking to God as a son would talk to his father, crying, "Father, Father, I love you! Father, Father, I have missed you! O Father, why did you go so far from me? Father, Father, I committed many sins, that was why you separated yourself from me." He began to cry. "Woe unto me, woe unto me, Father! What have I done? I have rebelled against you." He clapped one hand against the other, and started crying again: "But you are our Father! And a father should forgive his beloved son. Please, I entreat you. Forgive me, atone for me, pardon me." He struck his fist against his heart and heaved a great sigh, he cried and shouted. Suddenly he began to sing a sad melody. His voice was deep, the night dark, the valley deserted, and the sound echoed through the old olive trees. Unexpectedly, he grabbed Ezra by the hands and said to him, "Come Ezra. Come let us dance in honor of Father, in honor of our Father in heaven. How much happiness there is in the world! O how much happiness! How great is the happiness in His house!" He began to dance and dragged Ezra into his dance; spreading his arms, he threw his head back and enthusiastically burst forth, singing in the tune used by yeshiva students when studying Talmud: "Father, Father, always in happiness." The youth stopped abruptly, staring upwards for several moments. Ezra looked at him and saw his cheeks flushed and burning; his dark eyes had become even darker and deeper, and the veins in his neck bulged and he stood absolutely still. Then in a single motion, he turned around and said to Ezra, "we are going back. Come, let us return."

All this time Ezra had not uttered a word; he had observed the youth with no idea who this was in front of him. In all the synagogues of Jerusalem he had never seen prayer like this. He had once been worthy to see the afternoon prayer of the mystics in Jerusalem, the mystics of Beit El, as they stood without moving, crowned with their great tefillin, their heads buried in thick prayer books filled with special devotional prayers. But the prayer of this youth was different, entirely different. Nevertheless, it seemed to him that he had seen a spark of truth in his eyes; that the look on his face reflected what was in his soul, that his inner being matched his outward appearance; but still, he could not understand this type of worship. They walked in silence.

After several moments the youth turned to Ezra and said, "Do you not go to spiritual union with the blessed Creator? You are a God-fearing man and this is a positive mitzvah like the rest of the mitzvot, does it not say in the Torah, *cleave to Him?*"

Ezra replied to him: "I have heard from Haham Pinto that the sages ask, is it even possible for man to cleave to the Divine Presence? Rather one must adhere to His ways. Just as He repays kindness, you should also repay kindness; as He visits the sick so should you visit the sick. Thus one cleaves to the Divine Presence."

The Hasid stared at him and said, "May God have mercy upon you, Ezra, mercy upon you, for in your entire life you have never been worthy to attain true spiritual union in joy. How can a Jew live in the world without cleaving to Our Father in heaven? Do you actually think that someone who visits the sick or brings joy to the wretched attains spiritual union? How can this be cleaving? These are the precepts of kindness, and their goodness is very great, but I, I am not speaking about benevolence but about cleaving, when the soul that has descended to the very depths of the earth ascends to the heights of the heavens until it seems about to cleave to its very source. Although it knows that it will never reach it during its lifetime, the thirst continues to increase as it craves and longs for it."

Ezra said to him, "I do not know how to respond to you, but I have heard from Haham Pinto that we fulfill all the precepts according to the interpretations of our sages, and so they have explained this precept: You shall adhere to His ways."

The youth asked him, "And how did your rabbi interpret the precept to love the divine name, which Maimonides said is not bound to a man's heart until he is constantly absorbed in it? Do you people not daily recite *Shema, And thou shalt love the Lord thy God with all thine heart, and with all thy soul, and with all thy might?*"

Ezra replied, "I have never heard this explicitly in Haham Pinto's sermons, but on one occasion he read to us from the words of Maimonides about the proper way to love God, that when a person reflects upon the world with its wondrous creations he immediately experiences great love. He also told us that Maimonides specifically calls the book that treats the mitzvot of tefillin, mezuzah, circumcision, the recitation of *Shema*, prayer, and blessings, the *Book of Love*. But in general," Ezra added, "I am surprised that you, one who engages in spiritual union, should ask such a question. For how could someone observe the great kindnesses that He performs each day and not love Him?"

The youth would not let him alone, and continued to ask,

"Ezra, Ezra, you have given me many many answers from your rabbi, but mercy be upon you, mercy be upon you, Ezra, when your soul yearns and craves and thirsts for the living God until it is consumed with longing, what do you do? Where do you go?"

Ezra responded immediately, "To the book of Psalms."

Chapter eight

In which we leave the youth consumed with his yearning, and recount what befell Ezra in the episode of the Psalms in the Ahdut Yisrael Synagogue.

The book of Psalms, composed by King David of blessed memory, was very dear to Ezra Siman Tov. In times of sorrow and times of happiness he used to sit in the Ahdut Yisrael Synagogue in Mahane Yehudah and chant the psalms in a melody he had learned from his father, and his father, in turn, from his father. The psalter lay open before him as the hymns flowed from his mouth, and he was absorbed in the psalms as if he were in another world. During those moments he could neither see nor hear anything. Tears veiled his eyes, and the verses tumbled from his mouth of their own accord. His tears saturated the pages of the psalter. He was always astonished that King David, of blessed memory, knew precisely what he himself was feeling at that very moment, as if he had written his psalms for Ezra alone. Any time was suitable for the recitation of the psalms, but particularly the Holy Sabbath, following the early-afternoon service.

Then he sat himself down in the synagogue all alone and recited the psalms for the Sabbath day. He began, as was customary, with the psalm composed by King David in an alphabetical acrostic with eight verses for each letter:

> *Blessed are the pure of path who walk in the law of the Lord,*
> *As those that keep his testimonies and that seek him whole-heartedly.*
> *And those that do no iniquity, that walk in his ways.*

Until he finished the Psalm:

> *Wandering like a lost sheep, seek Thy servant, for I do not forget thy mitzvot.*

He had once heard from Haham Pinto that the beginning of this psalm was like the beginning of a man's life, *Blessed are the pure of path,* but what was his end? *Wandering like a lost sheep*; a person can only appeal to the loyal shepherd: *Seek Thy servant.*

Ezra joyfully chanted verse after verse according to the melody. In those moments he thought about events he had witnessed, sermons he had heard, and pleasing commentaries and ethical teachings. Thinking he was alone in the synagogue in those moments after the early-afternoon service, Ezra did not realize that sometimes the *avrech*, Reb Moishe Dovid, would come and sit down at one of the tables in another corner of the room. Reb Moishe Dovid sought a deserted place in order to study in great depth and immerse his thoughts in difficult legal matters, and he too had discovered the stillness of the Ahdut Yisrael Synagogue in Mahane Yehudah on Sabbath afternoons. Ezra would chant the hymns of the psalms while Reb Moishe Dovid split hairs about a profound problem in Tractate Ketubot, his finger moving of its own accord from right to left as if it were sketching out the course of Rabbenu Tam's argument in Tosafot and his debate with Rashi. Much as Ezra counted on his fingers the various spices of the incense offering in the Temple, or the different attributes of God in the prayer *True, firm, founded, established, just, and trustworthy,* or the eight verses that begin with the letter aleph in the psalm with the alphabetic acrostic, so Reb Moishe Dovid counted on his fingers all the difficulties Rabbenu Tam had with Rashi, one by one. As each was entirely immersed in his own world, neither noticed the presence of the other.

One Sabbath, after the reading of the portion *Now Korah took,* the two of them were seated in the Ahdut Yisrael Synagogue. Ezra Siman Tov was chanting the psalm with the alphabetic acrostic, as was his custom, and Moishe Dovid was reflecting. Reb Moishe Dovid was studying a difficult passage and could not elucidate it satisfactorily. The difficulties were extremely perplexing and it seemed beyond all explanation. Reb Moishe Dovid paced through the synagogue as he reviewed the entire section, both the passage from the Talmud and the opinions of the medieval commentators, again and again, hoping to find a solution. Yet the more he pondered, the greater the difficulties grew, piling upon one another and threatening to close the small opening before him. Reb Moishe Dovid was never frightened by difficult passages. To the contrary, he knew all too well that the greater the difficulty, the greater the happiness in discovering its solution—but this time he was almost ready to surrender. Reb Moishe Dovid had exerted himself to such an extent that it suddenly occurred to him that he had deprived himself of the Sabbath joy. He had once heard that a scholar accustomed to studying the most difficult passages in the Talmud during the week should read the homiletic passages on the Sabbath for his enjoyment, for if he grapples with the legal discussions in his usual manner, he will find himself desecrating the Sabbath. Reb Moishe Dovid had never accepted this teaching; for him, matters of Torah required deep and intense reflection, and intense labor over the Torah was an adornment to the Sabbath and a crown upon its head. Thoughts raced through his mind as he racked his brains. Did we not recite as children, "if you have labored and discovered, then you should believe,"—meaning, believe that you have actually labored; but if you have not discovered then do not think that you have actually labored. For the discovery comes only through labor and exhaustion; and even then, it comes only unexpectedly.

Reb Moishe Dovid continued to think with all his might, and began to feel something like the end of a thread in his hands, except it was the thinnest of strands; as soon as he felt it, it immediately disappeared. But he knew, if he could only catch hold of it, the entire passage would open up before him, and who knew, perhaps he would be worthy to discover a great new interpretation, which would be published in his name in the yeshiva's bi-annual journal of new insights into the Torah, and his reputation would be made.

The thin thread was nearly in his hands, brightness poised to pour onto his face, when suddenly he heard, in the emptiness of the deserted synagogue, a loud and clear voice chanting a melody, *Open Thou mine eyes, that I may behold wondrous things out of Thy law.* Then it returned and repeated with even greater force, *Open Thou mine eyes, that I may behold wondrous things out of Thy law,* and a third time, *Open Thou mine eyes, that I may behold wondrous things out of Thy law.* As the voice chanted, Reb Moishe Dovid became confused and the thin thread of his thought eluded him; he tried to catch hold of it, but it evaded him until finally it vanished. Exasperated by the voice, Reb Moishe Dovid went in search of it and found Ezra. He saw him sitting, his face aglow, the psalter in his hands, reading aloud.

Reb Moishe Dovid interrupted him and said, "Ezra, lower your voice and read quietly, for I am reflecting on a difficult passage in the Talmud and your recitation of the Psalms is confusing my thoughts. I had almost deciphered the passage when your singing disturbed and distracted me. I know all too well that the sages supposedly said that King David asked God that the recitation of his Psalms be as important as the study of the most difficult tractates in the Talmud. It is true that David made such a request, but the sages do not report if he received an answer from heaven or if God assented. Besides, you should know that the Torah was given for man to labor, not for his delight and enjoyment, that the Psalms were uttered with divine inspiration, not for someone to sing to himself after the Sabbath meal for his own pleasure."

Ezra stared in front of him and knew not what to say. For twenty years he had been reciting the psalms in the Ahdut Yisrael Synagogue in Mahane Yehudah, and had never once disturbed another person nor had anyone ever disturbed him. Was it possible for the Psalms of King David, of blessed memory, to disturb someone? Ezra remained silent and continued to recite the psalms in an undertone. But the pleasure he had felt grew faint and a single tear trickled from the corner of his eye down his cheek.

Every Sabbath after he recited the psalms he returned home and sat for a time with his wife, Madame Sarah, on the veranda, their sun-drenched porch. The veranda was surrounded by plants and aromatic herbs, roses, jasmine, and sweet peas climbed and descended from every corner, moderating the intense sunlight; containers of pickled vegetables, green cucumbers, small dark eggplants, and pink turnips with slivers of lemon, surrounded them on all sides. At that hour, as Madame Sarah sat by his side, caressed by the rays of the sun, and he told her the homilies of Haham Pinto, she looked at him, and there was tranquility between them.

That day when he returned home Madame Sarah could immediately see that something had happened. She recognized his facial expressions, she knew the character of his face on weekdays when he came home from the laundry, or when he returned from prayer at the Western Wall, or from reciting the psalms in the Ahdut Yisrael Synagogue. When the brightness in his face was dim she knew immediately that something had happened. But if he did not recount what had occurred, she would not implore him to tell her. She knew that if he refrained from telling her, he did so in order to guard his tongue. Just as he was vigilant not to recount gossip, so was she careful not to receive it, and all the more so on the Sabbath. So she sought to soothe him with conversation. She talked to him about his beloved grandson. She told him that the previous day she had collected him from the Talmud Torah. His teacher had come over to her and told her that her grandson had uttered a thought as clever as that of a scholar, and he had praised him in front of all the other students. The teacher had said, "I am an experienced teacher, for twenty-five years

I have been teaching children, I am the son of a teacher, as well as the grandson of a teacher, and I am telling you, he has the head of a scholar's scholar! His talents are apparent already in his youth. In the future this boy is destined to become a learned and clever scholar."

Ezra knew that Madame Sarah was trying to soothe him, and pretended to be soothed. "Good, good," he said to her, but to himself he added in an undertone, "let us hope the boy is not smitten with arrogance."

Chapter nine

In which we leave Madame Sarah comforting
her husband on the verandah and recount
what befell Ezra with his great brother-in-law,
Doctor Yehudah Tawil, and the Tabernacle of
Peace.

Every Saturday night, after reciting the blessing to mark
the conclusion of the Sabbath, Ezra Siman Tov and his wife used to
visit her elder brother, Doctor Yehudah Tawil, at his house in Rehavia. Together they would eat a meal in honor of King David and bid
farewell to the Sabbath bride, sip hot tea, and sing hymns about Elijah the Prophet. When they arrived at his house, they would sometimes find him pacing back and forth in the great room whose walls
were lined with books, holding a volume of Ibn Gabirol's poems in
front of him and declaiming them in a loud emphatic voice. Occasionally they found him sitting in his small study hunched over his
desk, which was piled with books and offprints, correcting and eras-
ing, writing and editing. Madame Sarah and her sister-in-law drank

glasses of hot tea and chatted idly, Ezra Siman Tov kept silent and gazed at the great volumes resting on their shelves, and Doctor Tawil remained absorbed in the pages of the books before him. Occasionally he would lift his head in agitation from the desk in front of him, turn to Ezra and say: "Ezra, listen my son." He would read a line from a difficult poem and say, "For seven days I have been trying to interpret this line, and only today was I able to understand it. What do you think about my insight? Did you understand?" He would rush through the explanation, mentioning only the highlights, and adding, "There is more here than what I have described to you, but now is not the right time to explain it all, and when the heart desires, time expires." But in his mind he would think to himself, Ezra is incapable of understanding anything that I have discovered anyway, for he has neither read nor studied, and knows nothing of scholarship or culture, he is a simple man.

Doctor Yehudah Tawil loved to hear stories, and Ezra Siman Tov knew how to tell them. Every time they came to visit, Doctor Tawil said to him, "Ezra, tell us a story for the conclusion of the Sabbath." With ease Ezra would recount a pleasant story told by Haham Zion Ventura or a sweet parable related by Haham Pinto or something that he himself had seen in Jerusalem; these stories praised the merits of the people of Israel, for we read in the midrash, the *Tanna de-bei Eliyahu*, that every Saturday night after the Sabbath, Elijah the prophet sits down and records the merits of Israel.

Doctor Tawil had read many books of tales, but Ezra's were different. Dr. Tawil's books told learned stories with stinging riddles and deep allusions; stories with words that pierced like swords, whose authors had reached the very depths of the soul. The tales recounted by Ezra were simple, they were gentle and had a certain generosity, and more than once Doctor Tawil had chuckled over them. Nevertheless he loved hearing them and his heart was drawn to them. He used to wonder to himself: these simple tales, tales that contain no wisdom, no knowledge, no craftsmanship, what is it that draws my heart to them so?

Once Doctor Tawil could no longer restrain himself and said

to Ezra, "But Ezra, is there no slander or complaint against the world in your heart? Have you never met, in all your days, a wicked person, a wicked friend, or a wicked neighbor? Or perhaps the evil urge, the evil eye, or gossip? Every storybook includes something about them, how is it possible that all the stories you tell are stories of goodness? Is the entire world good in your eyes? Is it not filled with deceit, falsehood, and hypocrisy, with those who pursue honor and those greedy for money? In all your life have you never seen these things?"

Ezra Siman Tov replied, "I do not know how to respond to you. What my eyes see, what my ears hear, and what my heart feels, this is what I recount." Then Ezra said to Doctor Tawil, "Listen to the following story which happened to me. I was on my way to deliver a package from the laundry to a particular customer in Nahalat Shiva. A man took hold of me by the coat and pleaded with me: 'The tenth, be the tenth man for a minyan.' I went through a doorway and found myself in a small pleasant synagogue. It had a low ceiling and was filled with memorial plaques and oil lamps. The congregants rose to recite the afternoon service, which was led by an old man who prayed at an unhurried pace. Not a single one of the members objected. It was obvious that they respected him. We finished the service, and the old man approached me. He asked if I could wait a few moments longer for a lesson in the Talmud so that they could recite the Rabbi's Kaddish after it. I agreed. I took a seat at the table with the other eight and the old man sat at its head. He read a few lines from the Talmud. I looked over the passage and realized they were concluding the tractate. I was gazing at the illumination of their faces, and the old man leading the lesson said: 'Thank God that we have merited, we have been worthy to conclude the entire Talmud.' They hummed a melody and sang: *The law of the Lord is perfect, restoring the soul; the testimony of the Lord is sure, making wise the simple.* Someone took out a few cookies and a bottle. The old man said, 'For many years we have been studying together, and, thank God, we have been deemed worthy. Hence, everyone should offer an insight for the glory of the Torah.' Each one of them said something. Then came my turn. The old man said, 'Behold, you were worthy to be with us to complete the minyan, you must also say something.' I thought for a moment and said to them: 'I am not a man of words nor am I a scholar who can offer insights into the Torah. I am a simple man. But I know how to tell a story. You are surely all asking yourselves, why has this man been deemed worthy to participate in our completion of the Talmud? I will tell you a story, and you will all see that the Holy One, Blessed be He, does not deprive anyone of his due. A young boy used to come home every day in the early evening after Talmud Torah. On his way home he would come to this synagogue to recite the afternoon prayer. After the service they used to sit down and study Talmud. The boy did not understand anything, but the rhythm of the passage drew his ear and from time to time he sat on the side to listen. Occasionally the old men would give him a piece of fruit or a stick of candy. Fifty years later the boy has grown up and become a man, and you who have been studying have completed the Talmud.' The men at the table said, 'But in Heaven they do not deprive anyone of his due. Why should the young boy be so deprived?' I responded that the Almighty had determined that that boy, now a man, should deliver a parcel to the synagogue, and that they should ask him to complete their minyan for the afternoon prayer, and he too would participate in the completion of the Talmud. I paused for a moment and said to them, 'I am that boy.'

"A pleasant story, is it not?" asked Ezra, and he added, "You see, the world is full of stories, but we must open our eyes in order to see them."

After they had eaten the meal of farewell to the Sabbath bride, they would recite the grace after meals. Ezra used to recite the grace after meals aloud, at a deliberate pace. After he had rinsed his fingertips with the concluding waters and dried them, he recited the psalm *The Lord is my shepherd, I shall not want*, opened the prayer book and read aloud, word by word, as if he were counting pearls, offered supplication and expressed his gratitude for the food that had been given to him with grace and *great mercy, for His kindness is everlasting*. At each and every blessing his wife Madame Sarah answered aloud, "Amen." He waited for her before he continued to the next blessing. He blessed the table upon which they had eaten, "May it be like the table of our forefather Abraham, of blessed memory: all who are hungry should be fed from it, all who are thirsty should be given to drink from it"; he blessed his host and his wife, "May they have numerous children and may their worldly possessions flourish close to home." Madame Sarah responded "Amen." He enunciated each and every request of the merciful God. Upon hearing each one, Madame Sarah answered "Amen."

Doctor Tawil would recite grace from memory, in an undertone, and after quickly finishing the blessing, he would turn to examine a book written by a very great scholar while waiting for Ezra Siman Tov to finish the final blessing. This evening, when he finished, Doctor Tawil suddenly lifted his head from the book and said to Ezra: "Ezra, in the grace after meals we recite, 'May the merciful one spread the Tabernacle of Solomon over us.' Why Solomon's Tabernacle and not David's? Do we not say, 'May the merciful one restore the fallen tabernacle of David'?"

Ezra remained silent and reflected: Indeed, that is a good question and I have never thought about it. It even occurred to him to ask Haham Pinto on the Sabbath after his homily, but suddenly he was taken aback by Doctor Tawil's laughter. "Ezra! Ezra! Look and see how it is written in the prayer book right in front of you, the Tabernacle of His peace not the Tabernacle of Solomon! You confused 'His peace' with 'Solomon' because they sound the same, but they are written differently. Do you not see the importance of a thorough knowledge of grammar?" And he thought, this naïve man so prolongs his recitation of the grace after meals, yet he cannot distinguish "His peace" and "Solomon." Ezra Siman Tov was troubled but said nothing.

Chapter ten

In which we leave Ezra's troubles in his heart
and recount the life story of the Doctor,
Yehudah Tawil, what befell him in his youth,
and, later in life, the embarrassing story of
Judah HaLevi's hymns at the University.

Usually Doctor Tawil relished the stinging sharpness of
an explanation, but this time he saw the face of his brother-in-law
Ezra Siman Tov blanch, and immediately regretted his witticism. He
gazed at the face of this innocent man and realized he truly loved
him and held him in great esteem. He began to wonder, what is it
about Ezra that I find so pleasing? He is not learned and does not
care about intellectual issues or even poetry, he is neither a scholar
nor an enlightened man, and I, my whole life I have spent among
erudite men and scorned the common people, I have valued most
those with trenchant and incisive minds. He fixed his eyes on his
sister, Madame Sarah, who was looking at her husband Ezra, and
marveled at the depth of the affection between them.

He remembered the days of old. When he was young he would devote day and night to his studies at the university, shut away in his room, seeking to decipher a difficult line in a poem of Ibn Gabirol. Once, his father, the Haham, was immersed in a difficult passage of Maimonides. His mother had sent his sister to deliver a tray of freshly baked *borekas* to her brother in the Bukharan quarter, and Haham Menashe Kahanof entered their home to speak with his father, the Haham, about an important matter. He opened with honorific greetings and an exchange on matters of Torah ensued as they drank from glasses of cold water on round brass plates and feasted on quince jam brought by the Haham's wife in a beautiful dish accompanied by a small silver spoon.

They spoke of the troubles and distress of the people of Israel; only after the conversation had wound its way from topic to topic did it arrive at its preordained subject, a proposal of marriage to the daughter of Haham Tawil, the maiden Sarah. In the course of their discussion what had been implicit at the outset gradually became clear: Haham Menashe wanted to propose Ezra Siman Tov, the launderer, as a groom for Sarah. With modest praise he mentioned that Ezra lived from the sweat of his own brow, that the rabbis had spoken of his great fear of heaven, that he had a pleasant face and was scrupulous in his observance of the precepts, that he was a man well loved by all, and, as the sages said, a man who is pleasing to his fellow men is pleasing to the Lord, that he set aside time for the study of Torah, that his prayer was pure. The issue might be agreeably resolved if the Haham consented, if heaven looked favorably upon it, for the match appeared to be a good one, a pleasing and acceptable outcome, woman and man were united by the Lord, would that the Creator bring this to fruition, would that the omens be good and favorable, would that husband and wife be found worthy for the Divine Presence to rest upon them.

Meanwhile the young Yehudah Tawil was lingering in his room, his door ajar and his curiosity piqued, and although he listened attentively he caught only snatches of their conversation. When he understood what they were speaking about, he became so agitated that he nearly fell from his chair. Ezra Siman Tov, the launderer, the intended groom for his sister Sarah? Was Sarah not the epitome of perfection, crowned with both wisdom and knowledge? And Ezra, what was special about him? Neither Torah, nor wisdom, nor distinguished lineage. Assuredly, he thought to himself, his father, the incisive Haham, would reject Haham Menashe outright, and maybe even rebuke him for daring to suggest such a match. But what was actually happening? He saw his father cordially receive Haham Menashe; consider the matter thoughtfully and carefully; ask Haham Menashe if Ezra was a good-hearted man, moderate and accommodating, and genuinely God fearing; invite Haham Menashe to come once more on Saturday night following the Sabbath, after he had observed Ezra at the Sabbath sermon of Haham Pinto; and part from him in peace after accompanying him to the gate of the courtyard.

Yehudah Tawil was deeply agitated; he closed the book in front of him with such force that it almost cracked the spine, he left his room and noisily slammed the door shut. Hurrying to his father he said to him: "Father, Ezra Siman Tov the launderer and Sarah? What has gotten into Haham Menashe's head?" He knew his father as a man who possessed a sharp and penetrating mind, as an incisive thinker who loved scholars and knew the virtues of his own daughter, and he was certain that his father would discuss the matter with him.

His father, Haham Tawil, raised his eyes, glared at him with contempt, and said to him: 'You be silent! Do not speak about this matter at all. *Mêle-toi de tes oignons!* Mind your own business!' He had never heard his father speak to him so. Humiliated, he fell silent and returned to his room. Before he entered his room, his father gazed at him fondly and seemed to mumble to himself, *The Lord desires thy heart.*

Many years had passed since then. Doctor Tawil observed the light that emanated from the face of his brother-in-law, Ezra Siman Tov, and his thoughts froze in astonishment. His eyes brimmed with tears and he saw Ezra's stories pass before him. For his entire life he had immersed himself in the worlds of the poets; engrossed in scholarship he had risen through the ranks until he was awarded with a doctorate. How much had he looked forward to that day, always imagining that when he had attained such a rank and published his own work the entire world would shake, but behold, what had he attained and what remained of his world? Thoughts flooded his mind, the days and years of his life passed before him like a shadow and a dream. Suddenly the words of the poet passed over his lips:

> *My youthful vigor cares but for itself.*
> *When will I my haughty spirit save?*

For more than thirty years he had been studying the medieval Hebrew poetry of Sepharad. In the morning he dispensed his wisdom at the university to advanced students; from the early afternoon until midnight he sat hunched over his work desk. He had set up a special room solely for the purpose of his work. It was adorned entirely with books. New ones stood in rows, arrayed according to their size, their subject, their gleaming bindings. Above them rested older books in crumbling bindings, and books not bound at all, only tied together by string. Above them, spread out in piles, lay notebooks and various offprints. It was clear he had taken them out for a moment to examine something and left them there at the time because of the pressures of his work. The room was dark. Even the windowsills were covered with notebooks and reams of editorial proofs from the printing house. A heavy wooden desk stood in the center of the room holding a massive clutter of books arranged in teetering towers. In one corner rested a volume of the Jerusalem Talmud and upon it lay a Byzantine festival prayer rite with its yellow cover, which in turn supported a Catalan festival prayer rite, and on the summit of the pile stood the small prayer book that had been printed in Venice using the Bomberg typeface in the year 1601, a year whose numerical value was equal to the verse *How fair are your tents, O Jacob,* according to the abbreviated computation. Next to them lay the book of prayers and hymns of the holy community of Syrian Jews in Aleppo. If so much as one book were to slip, the entire tower would come tumbling down.

In between these mountains of books his face appeared. With

a pencil in one hand, an eraser in the other, and his notebook in front of him, he wrote and erased, erased and wrote, underlining a passage in one book and writing a note in another. His expression was neither one of anger nor of levity, but that of a man engrossed in his affairs. Occasionally, in the midst of his work, upon finding a new source for an expression used by Ibn Gabirol or an interesting inflection of the Nagid, a smile spread across his face. For instance there was the time he examined the poem *The day when the dry land...* by HaLevi, and read the verse, "You have sunk into the depths, the steps of Anamith, the paces of Shulamith, their pleasant feet." Upon realizing that the word 'depths' referred to 'depths of the sea' rather than 'depths of deceit,' his face lit up. The entire day was like a festival for him.

Before him always lay volumes of the Bible and the Mishnah, the Babylonian and Jerusalem Talmuds, works of midrash and various concordances. He had one perpetual complaint against those who compiled concordances: since the time they had arrived in the world, they had eliminated the pleasure of identifying a reference within a hymn; gone was the distinction between someone truly well versed and someone well versed only through the power of a concordance. Nevertheless, he did not restrain himself from searching concordances, not in order to find the sources of a hymn, as his colleagues were wont to do, but to set his mind at ease that he had not overlooked anything.

Much as his heart filled with passion for his rigorous scholarly work, the poetry of Sepharad was the love of his youth. When he examined the penitential prayers of Moses Ibn Ezra, the penitential poet *par excellence*, or the sanctification hymns of HaLevi, the letters would blur before his eyes, and he would remember the Day of Atonement during his distant childhood in the town of Tedef, a few miles outside Aleppo. He recalled the ancient synagogue that had stood there since the days of the Second Temple. There was an ark from the time of Ezra the Scribe, upon which they took vows and oaths, while next to it they excommunicated members of the community. Whenever the synagogue took hold of his imagination his ears would immediately hear the twittering voices of children, dressed entirely in white, singing loudly:

> *God, listen to your paupers*
> *Mark well our prayers and hear*
> *Father to Your children*
> *Do not stop up your ear*

The entire congregation surrounded them, sitting atop leather cushions wrapped in orange and green silk that covered the engraved wooden benches, and groaned quietly, *Father to Your children, Do not stop up your ear.* On the third repetition, the cantors, who stood in front of the ark in gleaming white caftans, attempted unsuccessfully to teach the congregation how to carry a tune. The chief cantor stood in the middle, shaking his turbaned head at the futile attempts of the congregation as if to say: "You will be forgiven; I do not want to squander my own voice just yet. On the contrary, sing for yourselves as you like. In a little while, I will begin to sing the prayer of sanctification, and we will all see who here can sing like a cantor." After the public repetition of the prayer and the recitation of kaddish they sat down to sing the hymns for the Day of Atonement. He had been a little boy at the time, Yehudah Tawil, and did not understand the secrets of rhyming or the mysteries of poetic meter, but nevertheless he understood in his soul how the syllables were strung together like pearls in the voices of the congregation.

> *Heavenly sparks came to Thee to speak their praise,*
> *Entreating Thy compassion for those bowed down by sin.*
> *In reverence and awe of Thee do they direct their ways;*
> *Before Thy sacred throne they raise their thunderous din.*

Each word like a shard cut from a sapphire.

When he came subsequently to edit the poems of Ibn Gabirol in a critical edition, he remembered the banquet his grandfather, Rabbi Yehudah Tawil the Priest, would host for scholars and distinguished members of the congregation on the festival of Shavuot. This festive meal was called the feast of Azharot, in honor of the poems sung on Shavuot, and was hosted exclusively by the president of the community; all acknowledged his grandfather's right to host the meal year after year. An eminent figure in the community was Rabbi Yehudah Tawil. He was even important in the eyes of the gentiles. He had received a golden chain from the government, and wore it around his neck on festivals. Because of his great importance, he had been appointed the honorary consul of Argentina.

Wondrous stories were recounted about his cleverness, such as the one about a visitor who once arrived in Aleppo, the Minister of Posts of a certain country. The elders of Aleppo wanted to honor him and threw a banquet for him, to which they invited all the consuls. Haham Yehudah Tawil, the honorary consul of Argentina, was also invited. After dinner every consul rose to propose a toast to the distinguished guest in the language of the country he served. Each one was fitting and appropriate, and afterwards they all praised the speaker, but when the time came for Haham Tawil to propose a toast, he was perplexed. He had never known the language of the country to which he was a consul. He considered the matter for a moment, looked around, and remarked to himself: It seems to me that much as I do not know this other language, none of my friends appears to be a great expert either. He raised his glass and began speaking in the holy tongue: "*Blessed...are they that dwell in thy house; they shall continually praise thee. Selah.*" He continued to recite the entire psalm from memory, with emphasis and tones of surprise, wonder and astonishment; at each and every verse he turned to the invited minister, who nodded his head in acknowledgement. When he had finished, everyone nodded in agreement and clapped in applause. The Minister of Posts approached him, took his hand and said: Your words were more refined than all the others, and the sounds of your language sweeter to my ear than those of any other. Haham Tawil smiled and said to himself, What an ignoramus! Is there anyone more refined than David, the psalmist of Israel? Is there any language sweeter than the holy tongue?

What was the feast of the Azharot? A brown tablecloth would cover the table in the courtyard and upon it a white tablecloth embroidered with beautiful blue flowers would be spread. The table was always laden with delicacies in honor of the day; baklava dripping with honey, *Ruz b'asal* (rice and honey), *ma'moul* cookies filled with Aleppan pistachios and dipped in *Natif*, the sticky and sweet Aleppan paste. On the table were also pitchers of milk, jars of white yogurt, and flasks of *sharbat luz* (milk of white almonds). The pleasant aroma of the delicacies would mingle with the scent of the spices growing in the garden. Members of the community would sit in a circle while the grace of the festival poured over Yehudah Tawil's grandfather, and he would intone the Azharot of Ibn Gabirol:

> *I will utter words of wisdom sweet to the mouth and will guide the wayfarer in the right path.*

And the reader would recite:

> *Have pity on the poor, visit the sick, comfort the mourners, and bury the dead. The willow leaves, the goodly boughs of trees, the fair citron fruit and the palm branch.*

Old Haham Tawil would ask the youths to identify the number of precepts that had appeared in the verses as well as their individual sources, and each one would strain to display his ability until the congregation took up the recitation again:

> *May the Most High speedily gather His afflicted people and rebuild His Temple in Zion and bring our dead back to life.*
> *Then shall sinners in their evils melt, while the righteous sing and rejoice.*

The image of the redemption of Zion would appear before them. Hardly had the congregation reached the middle of the hymn, when cantor Haham Meir Nehmad would begin singing in a trilling voice, *Elijah the Prophet Opened*, the hymn preceding the afternoon prayers.

When Doctor Tawil was deemed worthy to ascend to Jerusalem and study the different meters of Sephardic poetry at the university, he did not need to measure every foot and vowel of a hymn like the rest of his fellow students. Instead he would sing the hymn to himself with the tune used in the synagogue, and immediately recognize the meter. When he sat with the other students, who were encountering the poems of Sepharad for the first time, he mocked them in his heart, as if to say, "What do they want with Ibn Gabirol? They have their modern poets." When he heard them read the poems without a tune and stumble through the vocalization—omitting the vowels, neglecting the stress marks, failing to pronounce the guttural letters—he felt as if they were robbing him of his own personal treasure. When he learned the principles of Sephardic poetry—the methods of prosody and versification, the techniques of rhyming and coupling, the meter and the metaphors, and the various other poetic adornments—he increased his love through knowledge. For through knowledge there will be love: if the learning is slight, the love will be small; and if vast, great will be the love. His new love mingled with his childhood love for the melodies that played in his soul.

When he became a scholar he was in thrall to the poetry of Sepharad with his entire mind and all his means. He spent months deciphering the meaning of a single verse of HaLevi, and entire years combing through manuscript fragments of newly discovered poems bearing the acrostic Yehudah or HaLevi. As much as a single verse in a stanza of HaLevi was precious, so the contemporary poems published in journals were worthless. These poems seemed to him like collections of words, without order or meaning. He did not like poems without rhyme schemes or an established meter, and the words of his learned friends who were partial to these poems were of no consequence. Although his own son showed him, in the most triumphant manner, what HaLevi had written in his philosophical treatise,

The Kuzari—that he preferred the poems in Scripture, which have no rhyme scheme or fixed meter, to formal poems, and wrote about the adoption of meter in Hebrew poetry: *But they mingled among the gentiles and learned their ways*—nevertheless, he remained unappeased. He used to say, are they writing biblical poetry nowadays?

As was the custom among the learned, he used to exchange ideas with his scholarly friends from time to time. Four important scholars of the poetry of Sepharad lived in his city. Although they seemed to be his closest friends, he bore a slight grudge against them. He was resentful that although they had not been raised on the Sephardic hymns from childhood, they still devoted themselves to their scholarly investigation. They boasted of their new interpretations of language and new discoveries of individual stanzas or even entire hymns in unknown manuscripts. In turn he bragged of his intuitive mind and ability to unearth the sources of hymns buried in the ancient midrash that had escaped them. While they drew upon reference works and scholarly research, he had only to remember the conversation at his grandfather's table. He thought the scholar who drew upon his instinct and the memories of his youth was greater than one who relied on a concordance. But, they retorted, an instinct was not science. He had a reply to this, but kept silent because of their status in the academy.

In those days Doctor Tawil was busy completing an edition of some poems by HaLevi that he himself had accidentally discovered stuck together in the binding of an old edition to a commentary on the Jerusalem Talmud, *The Gold of the Land.* He had laboriously peeled the pages of the binding apart, and strained his eyes to transcribe the poems. He slaved over each and every jot and tittle and compiled their sources and composed a commentary. The work had taken two whole years. All that remained was for him to set down the vocalization, and he was extremely punctilious about vocalization. In the manuscript one could not discern an *i* from an *e* or an *a* from an *o*. Once, a scholar had published a poem written by the Nagid and had placed an *a* instead of an *e* in a certain word. Doctor Tawil had composed a lengthy article entitled "The Anguish of the

A and the Essence of the *E*," and had demonstrated with examples from Scripture and the Mishnah that the word should be vocalized with an *e* rather than an *a*, chastising people for their neglect of grammar and even alluding to a letter by Bialik rebuking a certain writer for confusing his vowels. After the article had appeared he had distributed it amongst his colleagues, and it had been praised by many scholars. A while later another journal had published a short rejoinder by the original scholar, entitled "Mobile Grammar, Shifty Criticism." He wrote that Doctor Tawil need not have toiled to prove what was known to even the simplest schoolboy, but that the copy editor had made an error, the *e* had moved from one word to the next and become an *a*.

As a result of his immense exertion on his edition of HaLevi, he was exhausted. He wanted to pause for a bit. When scholars seek respite, they turn to words of wisdom. As it happened to be the Sabbath of Remembrance before the holiday of Purim, he began to peruse HaLevi's hymn, "O Lord Thy Mercy." His community in Aleppo had customarily recited this hymn before the reading of the Torah on the Sabbath of Remembrance, for it told the story of Esther in an alphabetic acrostic. When he reached the letter *w* he read: "Wonderful sayings whispered Esther the Queen." He remembered the Aleppo prayer book that contained two renditions of the verses for the letter W. The elders had recounted a story in explanation: When Rabbi Yehudah HaLevi was composing the poem "O Lord Thy Mercy" he simply could not think of a verse for the letter *w*. Although several possibilities had occurred to him, none found favor in his eyes. At that time, Rabbi Abraham Ibn Ezra, stricken by terrible poverty, was sojourning with HaLevi. When he heard of his host's pain, he wrote on a slip of paper "Wonderful sayings whispered Esther the Queen" and completed the verse. He tossed the note into the garden, and it was soon discovered by Rabbi Yehudah HaLevi. As the verses pleased him, he quickly incorporated them into the hymn. Yet his heart filled with misgivings, for one of the verses was not his own. Many years later he amended the poem and introduced a verse of his own in its place. Thus two versions for the letter *w* have been preserved in the hymn. One written by Rabbi Abraham Ibn Ezra:

> *Wonderful sayings whispered Esther the Queen*
> *Inscribed in a book in Mordecai's name*
> *Promoted was he and by everyone seen*
> *Hills and mountains recount his fame*

And one by Rabbi Yehudah HaLevi

> *Watching guards devised a plot*
> *To drop a drug in the royal cup*
> *One would watch the other not*
> *Until the king did sup*

There was a tradition in Aleppo, that one year they would recite the stanza by HaLevi and the next year the one by Ibn Ezra. At that moment, Doctor Tawil, whose many years of research had established an intimate bond between him and HaLevi, felt HaLevi's anguish. HaLevi, before whom the treasures of the language lay spread out like a beautiful dress, who had composed a lengthy hymn with verses threaded like pearls according to the scroll of Esther and its rabbinic interpretations, was missing a single stanza and needed to supplement it with a verse written by Ibn Ezra? With the passing of generations, people began to think that it too had been written by him.

As Doctor Tawil reflected on this story the idea for a prank suddenly took hold of him. Immediately he banished it from his thoughts and continued with his work. Except it refused to go away. He got up, walked four paces in his study and returned to his chair. Thoughts of the prank continued to pester him. He steeled himself to overcome his temptation: Am I a small child or a scholar of medieval poetry? But the thought would not let up. What was it that so plagued his mind? A Purim prank. His desires pleaded with him: How many stanzas have you written when the spirit has moved you, and how similar are they to the sacred hymns of HaLevi? In another few days the scholars you have invited will gather in your home to examine the cycle of poems by HaLevi. Let us amuse ourselves a bit in honor of Purim. Put a poem of your own amidst the new poems of HaLevi, and let us see if the scholars can detect whether it is HaLevi's or yours.

As much as he enjoyed the thought of the prank, he was shocked by the idea of such a forgery. He was surprised at himself that such an idea had even occurred to him. He arose and took down the book of hymns, *The Song of Israel,* by Rabbi Israel Najara, whose poems possessed a certain holiness and grace that enabled him to divert his attention from his desires. When he looked at the title of the volume, however, he did not read *The Songs of Israel,* but "The Poems of Yehudah Tawil." The words of his own poems appeared before him instead of Najara's petition, *Let Israel utter songs of praise to the awesome God.* He lay the book down on the desk and began to berate himself. Then he repeated to himself the rabbinic adage, that "one who becomes angry is as one who worships idols." He sat down again at his desk and tapped his fingers on it. He recalled the passage in the Talmud in Tractate Gittin about the gnat that went into Titus's nostril and burrowed its way to his brain and gnawed at it; only when it heard the blows of the blacksmith did it fall silent. But the gnat in his own mind refused to be silenced. On the contrary, his ears took the drumming of his fingers for the sounds of the vowels and the metrical feet of his own poem. He said to himself, now that it has occurred to me, I may as well scan the meter of the poem. He measured out the syllables and discovered the meter was precisely correct. He smiled to himself. He began to negotiate with his own desires but could not reach a conclusion. As is the way of the world, he finally yielded. He copied out his own poem onto a page similar to the ones on which he had transcribed HaLevi's and put the page among the cycle of poems. Once he had satisfied his own desires he returned to his work and finished it.

When the appointed day arrived, his four learned friends from the academy arrived at his home. They began to discuss politics and eventually turned to more learned issues, although he still had not told them the reason for their gathering. They began to argue about a new word recently invented by the Academy for Hebrew Language, about verbs with a guttural radical, about the foreign slang that ruled the streets of the land, the decline of the generations at the university, and the scarcity of students in medieval poetry. He served them Turkish coffee and dry Oriental *ka'ak* sprinkled with scented yellow sesame seeds. When he brought in the coffee, he chuckled. He realized he had startled them with his sudden laughter.

"I will recount to you the reason for my laughter," he said. "It was because of something that happened thirty years ago. When we ascended to the Land of Israel, we rented our home from a family of German lineage, enlightened and good-hearted people. They invited us to their home and received us in their beautiful mansion in a cordial fashion, with impeccable manners, the likes of which we had never seen before in Israel, similar to the hospitality of the Spaniards in Aleppo. After a few moments of conversation in French—and we relished the opportunity to speak the language once again—the hostess served chocolate cookies covered in cream. 'Would you like a cookie?' she asked us. We responded sheepishly, '*Non, merci*, there is no need. We have already eaten and are quite satiated.' She picked up the tray and took it back inside. We were astonished and angry. In our community in Aleppo a guest must first refuse any invitation. Only after the host insists three or four times can he acquiesce and allow himself to taste something. A host, after being rebuffed the first time, would never think the refusal genuine. But because we had refused her once, she took the cookies away. We continued to talk and they brought in coffee, this time without asking. This caused us even greater astonishment. Not because it was served in huge glass mugs with milk and sugar, as opposed to the bitter coffee we serve in small colorful earthenware cups, but because when a host in our community serves coffee he is subtly hinting that the visit has come to an end. We had assumed our custom was universally observed and were unversed in the ways of the world, of each place with its own particular customs. We truncated our conversation when we had thought to continue it; we feigned exhaustion, pointing to the stresses of the day, and returned home. This is the reason I laughed," said Doctor Tawil, "because of those memories. But now even I, a Syrian, bring coffee before we have even begun our conversation."

He let out a small sigh and said: "How many blunders would be avoided if one could learn the language of one's fellow man?" His friends nodded their heads as if to indicate their agreement, but he could detect signs of uneasiness in their faces. It seemed to him as if they were saying, "Yet again you are talking about Ashkenazim and Sephardim, something unbecoming to a man of scholarship like yourself." He said to himself, I imagined I saw something, but it was only in my mind, they were not thinking it. I was speaking from my heart, but they did not appreciate it. How many times had he had similar encounters in his scholarly work at the university, when he imagined that some tension had surfaced between him and those he was speaking with, but could never be certain if it were so. He knew all too well that Syrians were proud, even hypersensitive, and he always thought that he was imagining the entire episode. But he had never resolved his doubts. In those circumstances he used to tell an amusing story about Aleppo and its scholars, in order to dull the pain. Yet it seemed to him that not only did this fail to mollify his uneasiness, it made it even greater. In the very moment when he sought to repair something, he discovered it had only gotten worse.

One such instance had occurred when his great book on Ibn Gabirol appeared. Everyone had praised the work except for one scholar of Sephardic poetry, who had avoided him. When he next saw him, he had asked: "Does my book not appeal to His Honor?"

"It is a very pleasant book," the scholar had responded, "but not a scientific one." He had stopped there and not clarified his comment.

"In what way is it not a scholarly work? Does it not contain all the different variants from the manuscripts? Does it lack the standard scholarly apparatus? Did I not write an introduction, as is customary? Did I not describe all the manuscripts, stating the height and width in centimeters, indicate in which library each could be found and where one could examine a photocopy, identify the type of script employed by each scribe and where the texts were illegible? Did I not explain how various scholars mistook a poem by one author for that of another? In what way is it not scholarly?" Doctor Tawil had retorted.

"You have written a great work," had been the response, "it is well known that you worked very hard, it is a pleasant work. But not a scientific one."

Such an ambiguous statement from such a great scholar—to which he could not respond with any possible answer—had greatly exasperated him. From then on they had been hostile to one another. Even at that point Doctor Tawil had been plagued by doubts. I am a man of the East, a doctor, a Syrian, a lover of poetry and a pleasant man. I will never be a scholar. But then he would reply to himself: you see only your own uncertainties. Still, he had been unable to free his mind from misgivings. From time to time these doubts returned and stirred within him.

After his colleagues had partaken of the Oriental *ka'ak* he had put before them, he took out the collection of poems, stood up like a cantor and declaimed in a celebratory voice: "Teachers and scholars, colleagues and friends, before you are poems of Yehudah HaLevi that you have never laid eyes upon! If you should ask where I found them, I say, they were stuck together in the binding of a very old commentary on the Jerusalem Talmud, *The Gold of the Land*, which lay like a stone unturned in the Leningrad library."

One professor smiled; he had suspected that Doctor Tawil had discovered new hymns. On a number of recent occasions Doctor Tawil had sought his advice about an ambiguity relating to the vocalization of a particular word. The other three wore blank faces, so as not to reveal their surprise in public, heaven forefend, for scholars did not behave in such a fashion. A moment later their faces grew strained with the type of expression that comes from envy of the heart. Would it really be Doctor Tawil who would attain such an honor, and whose name would be known throughout the world? At first their eyes fell to the ground in anger, but soon happiness overtook their jealousy. After all, they were scholars of literature, and it was no trifling matter for the study of literature in our time for such a discovery to have been made. New poems by the most exalted of all poets! The revelation was cause for great celebration. Then their faces fell yet again. Twisted between jealousy and happiness, their smiles grew bitter. They considered the matter for a moment and said to themselves: Who can be so sure that they were really composed by HaLevi? At such a thought, their faces beamed once more.

Doctor Tawil, whom they had annoyed for years with the claim that his personal intuition was not an academic resource, read their thoughts. He opened the collection in front of him with pride wrapped in modesty and said, "Let our teachers, the masters of the study of poetry decide: HaLevi or not? Treasure or forgery? Teach me and I will be silent."

They all stood up and began to examine the poems. One scholar began and said, "It is well known that many poets incorporated an acrostic in their poems with the name Yehudah HaLevi in order to mislead their audience."

Another responded and said, "No, no, on the contrary, this is the language of HaLevi."

The third said "I do not recall HaLevi ever using this particular word."

In his great agitation Doctor Tawil forgot his manners. He jumped on a chair and drew from his library a notebook that he had prepared several years earlier, containing a concordance of all the words used by HaLevi in alphabetical order. As soon as he looked through it he discovered that the word in question appeared three times in HaLevi's famous cycle of poems on Zion. He was delighted that now he knew he had not labored in vain in preparing the concordance, even though he had never found anyone to publish it, and a foundation in America from whom he had solicited support had not even bothered to respond to his request. He did not wait for his colleagues to concede the truth aloud, but he knew they already did so in their hearts.

Thus the four scholars continued and argued with each other until the hour grew late. They thanked their host and stood up to take their leave. Doctor Tawil held them for a moment and said: "Gentleman, I have one other thing to say. A Purim prank. In this collection that you have just examined, which consists almost entirely of poems by HaLevi, there is one poem that I myself wrote."

They were all astonished, they grew embarrassed and angry. How could a learned scholar do such a thing? Then one of them began to laugh, and the rest gradually followed suit. They patted him on the back.

"Well done, Yehudah, well done," one of them said. "In your old age you amuse yourself with children's games. If this is so, perhaps all of the poems were written by you."

Another colleague turned to him. "Perhaps HaLevi revealed himself to you in a dream and recited the poems to you. He left you with a fitting style. You shall be our poet. Why even bother to waste your time in pursuit of scholarship?"

Thus they offered him words of praise as well as ridicule. And then they said in unison, "However, let the master show us the poem that we mistook for genuine."

Their closing words encouraged him. He opened the collection of poems and said: "At once I shall present the poem that confounded you and you supposed authentic." Leafing through the collection, he read poem after poem. The first one was by HaLevi, as was the second, and the third as well. He examined all of them but could not find his own poem. He went back and perused them again and began to stammer: "This cannot be. This simply cannot be. It is impossible that even I think my own poem was written by HaLevi." He thoroughly inspected poem after poem but could not find it. His cheeks grew pale, and he could not look at any of his colleagues in the eye. But they all gazed at him directly.

One of them began to speak. "You probably made a mistake. A celebrated scholar such as yourself would certainly not confuse one of his own poems with one by HaLevi. Perhaps you were exhausted from working so hard, or exceeded your own strength."

Another turned to him and said, "Undoubtedly you were just trying to make a joke. Except not everyone has the same sense of humor or the same taste. If you were seeking to entertain us, let us all laugh with you." He began to laugh.

One of them looked at his watch and said, "The last bus to our neighborhood departs in just a few minutes, and we must take our leave of you. We will certainly meet again at the grand reception that the academy will organize in your honor. There you can read to us from HaLevi's poems and perhaps you will even be worthy of composing a poem of your own."

Their words pierced his body like poisoned darts. They left him in peace and wished him good luck for his new publication. He responded with hurried thanks, but his eyes remained fixed to the ground as he accompanied them to the bus stop. In his heart he prayed for the bus to come quickly so he would not have to wait with them for any length of the time. But such is the way of the world, it is precisely when we want the bus to come immediately that it refuses to obey our will. He waited with them for a few minutes that felt to him like an entire day. They chatted amongst themselves about the new dean who had recently been chosen but he stood there as if he could not hear a word. As soon as the bus arrived he quickly returned home.

That night he slept not a wink. Not for the shame of humiliation before his colleagues but because he yearned for his own poem. It had been an outstanding poem, replete with images, ordered according to a rhyme scheme, and adhering to a strict meter. And it was his own. The matter was as clear to him as the afternoon sunshine. Had his mind become utterly confused? How could he have lost it amongst HaLevi's poems? You might think it was a great honor for him to imagine his own poem as a poem by the finest of the medieval poets. Nevertheless, whether an honor or not, he wanted to reclaim his own work, not to have it submerged under the work of others.

He went back to the book and read it from beginning to end and again from the end to the beginning. He separated the pages from one another, lest they had stuck together. But he could not find it. Tears brimmed in his eyes. Do I have nothing I can call my own? He put the book down and laid it aside. He was saddened by his embarrassment before his colleagues, but even more, he was disappointed with himself for yielding to temptation. He redoubled his labors in an attempt to forget the entire episode.

He diverted his attention from the entire affair and returned to his work preparing the collection of poems for publication. When he needed to go to the university to verify the notes in his book he endeavored not to cross paths with any of the colleagues who had been with him at the time of the incident. In the reading room he chose to sit at the last table, among those allocated for the general public, contrary to his custom of sitting at one of the reserved tables. In what way were the reserved tables so exceptional? Not by their own right, for in and of themselves they were similar to all the other tables in the reading room; rather because of the people who sat there, for they were reserved exclusively for the scholars of the university. Not to ensure there was enough space for them, for the reading room lacked not for space but for readers, but in order to distinguish between those who sat and read books for their own pleasure and those who sat and read books for the pursuit of scholarship and the benefit of others. Before he began his work he uttered a short prayer: would that not a soul sees me here. If one of his colleagues entered the room, he buried his head in his books as if he were busy at work and had no time for idle chatter. Nevertheless, nearly every time he went there he encountered one of his colleagues. Curtly he would acknowledge them, but they would linger with broad grins stretched across their faces and slap him on the back as if they were old friends. Their smiles seemed to him like mocking smirks, and he heard their greetings as if they were saying: Good morning, has the good sir composed a new hymn? Or has he found his own hymn that went missing? Although they never mentioned it explicitly, with each and every word he could detect an allusion to the incident. The smiles on their faces and the looks in their eyes seemed to be filled with scorn and pity. Again he would repeat to himself, I am only seeing the fears of my own imagination. But he could not rid his mind of doubt. And so he continued to torture himself about his folly, that a man of scholarship like himself had been seduced by his own desire for such mischief.

Several months later his edition of HaLevi's poems appeared in print. It created a great stir in the world of scholarship. Several publications commissioned reviews of the book. At the same time the university had to select the recipient of a prize established by the Department of Education and donated by a rich Sephardi for the support of scholarship on the cultural legacy of Sephardic Jews. The members of the committee convened and chose Doctor Tawil as the recipient of the prize. They held a reception in his honor. All the members gathered and each delivered an address praising him. The president of the academy even appeared and offered a tribute to Doctor Tawil and other such scholars. He went on to extol the cultural legacy of Sephardim and the scholarly study of that culture. Turning to Doctor Tawil, he said he would be worthy of any such prize, as the son of an Oriental family who had ascended to the Land from Aleppo in his youth, and had progressed and excelled until he had even published a work of scholarship.

When Doctor Tawil listened to the president of the academy, it was if he heard him say: even though he had emigrated from Aleppo in his youth, he had still advanced and attained success. His cheeks turned pale and he cleared a cough from his throat, as if to ask, how are my origins at all relevant to my work? He felt the same tension he usually felt at such gatherings. It seemed to him as if they were saying, in these times, if you want to win an award, all you have to do is be Sephardi or write on their cultural legacy. Again he repeated to himself, I am only seeing the fears of my own imagination. Nevertheless, he could not rid his mind of doubt. As is the way of the world, however, the celebratory gatherings held in honor of his new book dimmed his thoughts of the earlier incident.

A year later, on the Sabbath of Remembrance, he opened the Aleppo community's book of hymns, as was his custom, in order to read the hymn, "O Lord thy Mercy." When he arrived at the letter W, "Wonderful sayings whispered Esther the Queen," he saw a piece of paper. He turned it over and found his own poem written on the page. He remembered the entire incident of the year before and understood that he had meant to put his own poem among the new poems by HaLevi but had forgotten it in the book of hymns. His expression, neither one of anger nor of levity, but that of a man deeply immersed in his work, changed to a wry smile, the same countenance he had worn when he discovered that the phrase in HaLevi's poem *The day when the dry land* referred not to the depths of deceit but to the depths of the sea.

Ever since that incident his mind had been confused, and he could find no respite in life. He immersed himself more and more in his work and kept apart from other people. Strange thoughts intruded upon him from afar and disrupted his peace of mind. On occasion, the image of his father, the Haham, appeared before him, standing before a volume of Maimonides, and then suddenly scornful laughter would burst forth from the mouths of his erudite colleagues and assault him as they professed their superiority over him. Then the vision of his father reading would return to him. At times the figure of Rahamim, the blind musician, appeared to him. Rahamim would play the violin, and he would flee, only to be pursued by the violin's melody calling out to him: "What have you done? What have you done?" But he felt bewildered: how could a melody chase a human being?

Doctor Tawil seemed suddenly to have woken from a dream. He found himself at the entrance to his house, with his brother-in-law Ezra Siman Tov standing before him. He felt deep love for Ezra but then remembered he had embarrassed him and was ashamed. He sought to make amends to him but knew not what to do. He laid his hand affectionately on Ezra's shoulder as if to tell him something, but knew not what to say. Bewildered, he lowered his eyes and turned to him: "Have a good week Ezra, have a good week and be blessed." On the table before him stood a pile of offprints sent to him by his learned colleagues. Such was the custom of professors at the university, when one published an article he sent an individual offprint of it to each of his colleagues. He picked up one of the articles on the table and gave it to Ezra. He stole a hurried glance at the title of the article he had given him: "Further investigations into the earlier meanings of the Aramaic phrase: *'The Lord desires thy heart.'*"

Chapter eleven

In which we take leave of Doctor Tawil
seeking to conciliate Ezra at his Rehavia home
and recount the tale of the *avrech* Moishe
Dovid who wanted to compose a great work
of Talmudic interpretations.

The night following Simhat Torah, the *avrech*, Reb Moishe
Dovid, sat in the house of study with the Talmudic tractate Sukkah
open before him. He was filled with delight, happy that he had been
worthy to celebrate the joy of Torah and pleased that the congregation had honored him as the Bridegroom of the Torah. In his heart
he said to himself: It would be impossible for me not to admit that I
am somewhat worthy of such an honor. For twenty-four years I have
studied Torah: at primary school, upper school, and in the great academy. Thank God, I have neither toiled in vain nor passed my days
idly. I have studied several tractates of the Talmud in their entirety
and even examined the subsequent rabbinic legal decisions on their
subjects. The most celebrated elders of the generation authorized my

permit to officiate as a rabbi, and I am known throughout the academy as one who can be consulted on any matter. Not that I have an adequate response to every single inquiry, rather I listen carefully to the issue, debate with the questioner, and through the dialectic of our argument the problem is clarified. What is more, I have established new interpretations of the Talmud. Behold, right here with me I have a collection of glosses to Tractates Ketubot and Yevamot, notes compiled in the margins of Tractate Kiddushin, and lectures for Tractate Bava Kamma. My interpretations in my little notebooks are like fine goods in small parcels, containing hundreds of brief insights in alphabetical order. I thank God for endowing me with wisdom and keeping me from the company of idlers. The time has now come for me to compose a work, especially now that it is winter, for the winter is a fitting time for an author: when the entire world is drenched by sorrowful rains, the author sits ensconced in his study, warmed by the heat of his stove, writing his interpretations.

His worthy thoughts led directly to action, and he sought to encourage himself. Zeal was fitting for a religious duty, for as soon as one seeks to fulfill a mitzvah the evil inclination seeks to take it away from him. *Therefore the zealous do their religious duty betimes.* Before the wretched one can dissuade them.

From the story thus far you already know that Reb Moishe Dovid regularly frequented the house of study. For twenty-four years he had occupied himself with the study of Talmud, had sought knowledge and refined his character. All his days he had used his good will to frustrate his evil inclination and to battle against the vices of arrogance and pride that ensnare all men, especially the learned. He had fought and won. To only one desire had he yielded. It seemed as if he had never resisted it at all, for it was a pure, even innocent wish; that is to say, one only for the sake of the study of Torah—the desire to create his own work. Reb Moishe Dovid was a lover of books. He spent hours upon hours every day in the library adjacent to the house of study. In each and every book he perused the introduction, read the scholarly approbations, the notices of the printers, the omissions mandated by the censor, the glosses that the author's son had included to avoid empty space in the final pages, and the responses of the critics.

On every Sabbath eve the desire to write his own work greatly intensified. Every Friday yeshiva students used to fulfill the saying in the Torah: *On the sixth day they shall prepare that which they bring in—* as the sages had interpreted it, that one who has labored on the day before the Sabbath shall eat on the Sabbath. They would spend most of their day performing mundane duties: laundering their clothes, binding their books, trimming their beards, glancing at the political columns in the weekend supplement paper, and doing various other chores in preparation for the Sabbath. As the better part of the day was spent in vain they surrendered the remaining few hours and did not go to the house of study. Since his colleagues did not attend the house of study on the Sabbath eve, Reb Moishe Dovid avoided it as well, for it was beneath his dignity to sit and engage in the study of Talmud all alone. The sages had once said: "What is the meaning of the verse *A sword is upon the liars and they shall become fools?* If scholars study one by one, then a sword hangs over the necks of the 'ones' who sit and study the Talmud all alone." Yet he did not want to engage in profane tasks, for they cause one to forget the words of Talmud. Therefore, every Friday, Reb Moishe Dovid went to the old bookseller. He remained there well past midday, taking down books, examining them, scrutinizing the binding, reading the introductions, studying a particular insight, testing its argument or finding corroboration. Each time he picked up a book, however, the desire to write his own work grew stronger within him.

That night, after Simhat Torah, his desire to write a book was even greater than usual. Exhausted from the festivities of that day, he said to himself, I shall rest tonight, and tomorrow I shall begin the work. As he recited the *Shema* before retiring he concentrated intently when he reached the verse *Take to heart these instructions with which I charge thee this day.* He rose the next dawn and prayed with the pious, for he who prays at sunrise is happy the entire day, and happiness is a unique precondition for innovation in the study of Talmud. After the service he arranged his room for writing, organizing his implements to ensure they would be at his disposal as soon as he needed them. He put down several pencils, so that if the point of one should break he could immediately use another, for before he had time to sharpen the tip of the pencil he might lose the precise argument that had come to mind, as the thread of his thoughts was extremely fine, so fine that it required all the powers of his concentration. He took two notebooks, three or four sheets of large white paper, two rulers, an eraser, cylinders of adhesive tape, a stapler, and also a set of compasses; in the event that an insight into the laws of cultivating hybrids came to mind, he would be able to sketch an agricultural diagram next to his other investigations. He sat at his desk and arranged everything in front of him. He placed the pencils and the rulers to his right, the eraser to his left, and spread out the sheets of white paper on the desk as if they were a tablecloth.

He took down a copy of the Tanakh from the shelf in the room. If he needed to cite a verse from the Torah he could do so in its proper form, unlike the many learned scholars who cite biblical verses from the Talmud, garbling the verses. In addition he took a miniature set of the Talmud and put it in front of him. Next to it he placed Maimonides' code of the law, the *Yad Hazakah*, for most of his insights used this work as their starting point. Of the ancient commentaries to the Talmud, he put the glosses of Nahmanides and Ibn Adret on the table; of the modern commentaries, the book *The Expositions on the Book of Education*, the glosses of his eminence Rabbi Akiva Eiger, and the responsa of Rabbi Moses Sofer. Finally he returned to the library and withdrew a book of ethical teachings called *Nefesh HaHaim* by Rabbi Haim of Volozhin, which he studied for a short while before writing, in order to fulfill the Scriptural verse, *The fear of the Lord is the beginning of wisdom*. He also withdrew *Sha'are Teshuvah*, written by the pietist Rabbenu Jonah of Gerona, which teaches humility and confession; if he were worthy of a new insight into the Talmud, then he would guard against pride by reading a chapter of rebuke, as it is written: "From the marvel and wonder that is man's lot at the peak of his life, he shall watch his strength diminish and decrease, but he will not understand that he approaches his end with each passing day," and various other passages that shatter the arrogance of man.

After he had prepared his table he looked for a chair. Although he was not usually very particular about where he sat, an ordinary chair was nothing like a writer's chair. He replaced the lamp in front of him with another, for an ordinary lamp was nothing like a writer's lamp. After he had set all this up, his mind was at ease. He took his pencil in hand and readied himself to write.

A breeze suddenly blew through the open window and scattered his papers. He saw what had happened and remembered that he had once read in a scholarly approbation to a new book: "May the matters contained within this book be accepted by scholars and be scattered throughout the house of study." He thought to himself, it is a good omen that my words shall be scattered throughout the house of study like these pages are scattered throughout my room. He bent down and gathered all of the papers. A second breeze came and his papers blew in his face. He rose and shut the window. A small wrinkled piece of paper fell out of his volume of the Talmud. He unfolded it and read in the beautiful handwriting of a scribe: *Illumine our eyes in Thy Torah.* He smiled. He remembered writing the note in his youth. And why had he written it? To place on the page in front of him; when tempted by desire to abandon his efforts, he used to look at the note and immediately return to them. He did not neglect his study, but neither did his desire forsake its work of temptation. He said to himself: The sages said, desire attempts to conquer man each and every day, but how do I avoid my temptation? I fill myself with information. He continued talking to himself, carrying on a theoretical discussion in his head: If one is unwilling to distract himself with idle nonsense, he should divert himself with matters related to the Talmud. But is it actually possible for a person to distract himself when thinking about the Talmud? Certainly. For example, when one thinks about the proper method of study, which tractate to begin with, when to conclude the tractate and begin the next one, and other such matters relating to the study of Talmud.

He began to reflect. He stirred himself. He stared at the note in front of him and again read what was written: *Illumine our eyes in Thy Torah.* He justified his own desires to himself: most people waste their time with nonsense but you distract yourself with the study of Talmud, and even in your abrogation you continue to fulfill it. These thoughts penetrated deep into his heart. Although he had a proper retort, when temptation begins its conquest of someone's will, he can no longer respond. If he were to counter with a single objection, the temptation would immediately respond with a host of justifications, and either way he would find himself neglecting his study. When Reb Moishe Dovid perceived this, he said to himself, all my utterances are Torah, as it says, *that bringeth forth his fruit in his season, his leaf also shall not whither,* and our sages interpreted the verse, "even the everyday prattle of scholars merits study."

In any case, at this point three hours had passed. He said, "The time has come to eat breakfast, a meal that expands the mind, sets the heart at ease, and rescues one from error. If it achieves this for the common man, how much more so for the author of a great work." After he had eaten, he said, "Now I shall rest for a bit." He laid his head on the cushion and dozed off.

While he was napping, he had a dream. In his dream he was standing beside a printing press. As the scent of the press filled the air, folio upon folio of paper emerged from the press. Each folio contained eight pages. On each and every page there were square letters, the rounded letters known as Rashi script, and small letters to indicate a footnote, as well as triangular letters that had been used to print Rashi's explanation of a passage in Bava Metzia describing chunks of meat and fish that had already been chewed, and cursive letters. Although only Sephardi sages wrote in cursive script,' and although neither he nor anyone in his family was Sephardi—except for a single relative who had married his cousin—the sages said that no dream is devoid of insignificant details. There were large letters to indicate abbreviations, and at the top of every page there was a citation from the psalm with the alphabetic acrostic, *Were not thy Torah my delight, I would have perished in my affliction, O how I love thy Torah, it is my study all day long,* and other such verses in praise of the Torah. Standing by the press, he seized a folio proprietarily, as if to tell the workers: I take what is already mine. He shook his head, "Ehhh! This is a wonderful insight. *Every man shall kiss the lips that giveth a right answer.* Yet this one, I wish I could have removed it from the work, for I have found a refutation from a Mishnah in Tractate Negaim. On second thought, it contains such wonderful casuistry, and anyway not everyone is well versed in Tractate Negaim or the Mishnah."

His thumb realized he was splitting hairs and began to gyrate on its own accord, upwards and downwards as if he were actually studying the Talmud, in order to fulfill the verse in scripture, *With all my bones I shall say: Lord who is like unto thee?* Suddenly his thumb crashed into the table. Abruptly he awoke. He realized that he had fallen asleep and just woken up. "The time has come to write," he said. Taking a sheet of paper, he composed the following phrase in his head, "Law of the Order and Rule of the Discussion," in order to begin with the initials of the LORD, a sure sign of success. When he examined what he had composed, he was not pleased, for the sentence lacked proper structure, Order does not have a Law, and the Discussion does not have a Rule, and the word for Rule was in Aramaic, unfit for combination with Hebrew. He picked up his eraser and rubbed it out. He said to himself, I could have begun, "Principle of Principles and Pillar of the Sciences," but Maimonides preempted me in the opening words of his code. Or I could have written "Basis of Piety and Root of the Service," but Rabbi Moses Haim Luzzatto already used that as the opening for his work *The Path of the Just.* He picked up his pen, wrote a stroke of the letter Y at the top of the page, left a small space blank and said, "When I have reached a decision, I shall fill it in."

He saw that it was good, and said, "Now it is time to write the introduction." Once again, he began to split hairs. When his thumb realized he was engaging in dialectic, it began to move of its own accord, upwards and downwards. "What type of introduction should I write?" He mused, "If it is long, the learned will say, 'Alas, he expended so much effort and went to such lengths in his introduction but we have not seen it bear fruit.' But it cannot be short, for many scholars never examine the contents of a book but look only at the introduction. There are those who prolong their prayer, and when the prayer leader observes such lengthening he decides to extend his public repetition. When they see him do so, they pick up a book, turn to the introduction and begin to read. Consider the importance of this introduction in heaven: the people of Israel will peruse it when they expiate themselves before their Creator, during the eighteen benedictions and the public recitation of the Torah. Besides, in an introduction a writer demonstrates his poetic abilities, reveals the sentiments in his heart, displays the precision of his language and the purity of his style, rhymes in a short poem adorned with biblical citations and rabbinic aphorisms, expresses gratitude to those who supported him, and composes verse about the decline in generations, the lack of scholarship, the desecration of the Name, the question of fate, the longing for redemption, the restoration of the Divine Presence to Zion and the rebuilding of the Temple, and the like. And finally, the most crucial point, to conclude the introduction, I am forever grateful to the mistress of my house, may she live in peace, what's mine and yours is hers."

As he remembered his wife, he thought to himself how many sacrifices she had made to enable his study of Talmud, how much toil had she expended over his little ones, how much she had worried when he arrived late after spending time in the realm of scholars. When her mother had asked to her, "But how long, how long will this one remain in the house of study?" she responded, "Were he to listen to me, he would stay there all his days." When her mother had pressed her, asking "What exactly does he do there? Is he writing books or just drinking cups of tea with lemon?" she was pained and remained silent. Pained for the sake of her husband, silent out of respect for her mother. He thought to himself, now I shall reward her with a work she can show off to her mother and her friends, saying "Look at the book that we have written," using the plural "we". For what's mine and yours is hers.

He picked up his pen and, leaving the entire page blank,

wrote at the end: "What's mine and yours—is hers." He looked at what he had written, took his eraser and rubbed out the dash. He wrote instead in large square letters, "What's mine and yours is hers." Again he erased it and wrote, this time in Rashi script, "What's mine and yours is hers." Suddenly he had doubts. Should he have written, "What's yours and mine is hers."? It pained him that he could not remember. He knew the phrase came from the story about Rabbi Akiva and Rachel, the daughter of Kalba Savua. He even knew that the story appeared in Tractate Ketubot. But he could not recall the chapter or the page. Such is the manner of study these days, they keep a record of the page numbers of only the most difficult legal passages. If you were to ask any yeshiva student where the Tosafists mention Maimonides, they would immediately respond: Tractate Menahot, page forty-two, recto. But they skip the narrative passages, reasoning that stories were only included in the Talmud to amuse simple folk or scholars of midrash, but not for those inquiring into the depths of the law. Since he could not remember, he left it as it stood. He said, if it is correct, all the better. If not, the critics will say I altered the citation to refine the language. He went back and wrote: "What's mine and yours is hers."

The door opened and his wife tiptoed in to avoid disturbing him. Embarrassed, he covered the sheet of paper with a book. "It is time to eat," she whispered. After collecting his papers and laying down his pen, he rose to eat. He ate his fill and with each and every bite he directed his mind towards heaven, as it was written in the *Shulhan Aruch*, in paragraph two hundred and thirty one, "All of a man's actions should be for the sake of heaven." He intended that his eating should enable him to serve the Lord, specifically, to discover insights that his spirit had already received at Sinai and use them in his book. He recited the grace after meals and focused intently when he reached the verse *And Thy teaching that Thou hast taught us.* Having eaten, he went to take his afternoon nap, and although in the *Shulhan Aruch* our master had ruled against sleeping more than sixty breaths, the sleep of a horse, recent commentators had mitigated the ruling by establishing that sixty breaths were equivalent to more than two hours. What is more, bodies had grown weaker, and moreover he was extremely diligent and studied at night, for night was auspicious for the study of Torah, especially writing a book.

After waking from his slumber he approached his desk and said, what type of work shall I write? Not one like those composed by the learned nowadays. For the learned in these times write books about the most difficult Talmudic passages in the Order *Nashim* or the Order *Nezikin*. They select for themselves a few segments, mention the views held by several of the Ancients, pose questions about those views based on the inquiries of the Moderns, ascend to the heavens, descend to the depths, and then, reproducing an idea formulated by one of the luminaries of the generation and foundational pillars of Jewish law, they attach their entire discussion to the passage at hand. No such book would he compose, for such books languish in libraries and in the study halls of the great academies; there is no need for them. He who seeks to achieve basic familiarity with the entire Talmud has no use for them, while he who analyzes a single passage to such a great extent that he might actually read such a book instead studies the glosses of Nahmanides or Ibn Adret or analyzes a section of Maimonides until he clarifies the passage. And one who hopes to study every single book will complete his days before he completes the books. If he wishes to sharpen his mind with the logical erudition of the Moderns, he can simply turn to the works of our greatest rabbis: *The Ends of the Breastplate, Expositions on the Book of Education* and the like. If he wants to think about a more recent idea, better a small one of his own than a larger one belonging to someone else. Reb Moishe Dovid admitted to himself that he too felt this way, although not out of any particular love for himself, for he was a learned man with the most refined manners. Rather, there was good reason for his feelings: the writings of his colleagues had been collected and published as a book; his own had not yet been written, and perhaps he would be worthy to discover the truth of Torah, receive some assistance, collect some money, and publish his very own book.

He would not compose such a work, nor would he do the work of a collector, for some collect and document each and every issue in the Talmud but rid the passages of their vitality and omit the questions and responses. Those books contain not the slightest hint of any innovation or dialectic. The work he was going to compose would include new interpretations in Jewish law, an elucidation of the principal issues in a given passage, textual variants, and clever commentary to amuse the reader. Learned rabbis would consider his analysis, young students would turn to his book for a summary of the passage they had studied, and academics would re-examine their textual variants, all who used it would find what they sought.

"Now it is time to write," he said. He picked up the notebooks before him. Examining his insights into Tractate Ketubot, he realized they followed the dialectical method. That year a particularly clever rabbi had come to the academy and attracted all the students to his method, and all of his own notes for the year followed the dialectical method. They were not right for a longer work. Opening his notebook to Tractate Yevamot he saw that here his observations were arranged according to the order of the passages and contained nothing of the innovative dialectic. He found annotations he had made in the margin to Tractate Bava Batra. He investigated them. One of his insights had already been discussed in the book *The Face of Joshua*, and another erudite note about a textual variant was already included in the great compilation of manuscript variants written by R. Nathan Neta Rabinovitch, *The Finer Points of the Scribes*. From his files he pulled out a sheaf of papers he had written on Tractate Bava Kamma, but soon realized the greater part of them contained notes on the lectures he had heard from his rabbi, and although he had added his own personal flourishes, how could he publish them in his own name? If he were to quote them in his rabbi's name, his rabbi might as well write his own work and include in the margin, "I owe this observation to my devoted student." In sum, he found some grounds to disqualify each and every insight from being worthy of his composition.

He wrinkled his brow in an effort to remember the thousands of ideas he had conceived over the twenty-four years he had studied in yeshiva and the academy, ideas about the tractates of the Talmud and the legal decisions of the Ancients and the Moderns, but he could not remember a single one. He gave a few coins to charity and recited the *Ten Sons of Rav Pappa*, a prayer that was declaimed at the conclusion of a tractate and was supposed to prevent forgetfulness, but still he could not remember his ideas. He examined the work of Maimonides, but not a single innovative thought came to him. He opened several books by the Moderns, but because of their great depth and erudition he could not follow their arguments, and though he tried hard, he could not grasp their reasoning and nothing entered his mind.

He realized that he could not come up with anything. He looked down at his desk sadly, and saw that on the entire page he had not written more than a stroke of the letter Y. His lowered eyes brimmed with tears. He picked up the books of Rabbi Akiva Eiger and *The Expositions on the Book of Education* and returned them to the bookshelf. He closed the volumes of the Talmud and Maimonides, picked them up and put them in their proper places. He gathered up the sheets of white paper and removed them from the table. Setting his elbows on top of his empty desk, he rested his head upon his hands and burst into tears: My insights, where are you? My theories, where have you gone? Nights that my eyes felt no sleep, days that I stirred not from the tent of Torah, where is the suffering I suffered, the labor I labored, the toil I toiled?

Through his tears he remembered that his neighbor the launderer, Ezra Siman Tov, used to recite with a beautiful melody the psalms of King David, may his memory be blessed, following the early-afternoon service in the Ahdut Yisrael Synagogue in Mahane Yehudah, and that he had taken great pleasure in them at the same time as Reb Moishe Dovid studied the Talmud and the Tosafists in great depth. Once, he remembered, he had rebuked Ezra Siman Tov, saying that his recitation of the psalms disturbed the learned in their study, and demanded that he lower his voice and read quietly. Now the melody of the psalms sung by Ezra Siman Tov was ringing in his ears. He paused for a few moments but Ezra's tune refused to let him go. He tried to clear his mind but the tune kept echoing through his head; in fact, it grew stronger and stronger. Finally he stood up from his seat, took a small volume of Psalms, set it down on his empty desk, and opened to the alphabetic acrostic written by King David, of blessed memory, in praise of the Torah. He began to tremble and cry out in Ezra Siman Tov's melody:

All they that keep His testimonies and that seek Him with whole heart are blessed. Also they that do no iniquity, that walk in His ways. He continued to chant. When he reached the letter O and the verse *Open Thou mine eyes, that I may behold wondrous things out of Thy law,* the tune arose within him of its own accord. *Open Thou mine eyes, that I may behold wondrous things out of Thy law.* The verse was very pleasing to him. He repeated it a second time: *Open Thou mine eyes, that I may behold wondrous things out of Thy law.* And then a third time: *Open Thou mine eyes, that I may behold wondrous things out of Thy law.* With each and every repetition his face glowed with greater devotion, until his entire body trembled. If the next verse had not pulled him forward, *Only a sojourner am I in the land, do not hide Thy mitzvot from me,* he would not have abandoned the previous one.

Thus he continued verse after verse. With each and every one he experienced sensations he had never felt before, until finally he asked himself in bewilderment: these verses, where have they come from? I have truly never seen them in my life. He concluded the entire acrostic, kissed the miniature psalter with tenderness and put it down on his desk. He picked up the Mishnah with Obadiah of Bertinoro's commentary. Opening with the very first chapter of the very first tractate, Tractate Berachot, he chanted the mishnah: *From what time in the evening may the* Shema *be recited? From the time when the priests enter the Temple to eat of their Heave-offering until the end of the first watch,* and Bertinoro's comment: *the first watch,* for the night is divided into three watches. He continued to recite: *From what time in the morning may the* Shema *be recited?* and followed it with Bertinoro's comment. He understood the words of the Mishnah as he had never understood them before. He said to himself, the words of this mishnah, where have they come from? He went back and repeated the mishnah with Bertinoro's comments a second time.

After concluding the entire chapter he repeated it several times until he knew it by heart. He closed the book and tested himself. *From what time in the evening?* until the end of the chapter, just like a schoolboy. Remembering the question in the Talmud, *What authority has the mishnah that the* Shema *is to be read at all that it raises the question: From what time?*, he went to his library, took down a small volume of the Talmud, put it in front of him, opened Tractate Berachot and joyfully studied the entire first page with Rashi's commentary. He looked at Rashi's comment to the phrase, *for all offerings that must be consumed 'the same day'* and knew that Maimonides disagreed with Rashi. He took Maimonides' Code of Law, *Yad Hazakah*, and placed it to his right. Examining the paragraph of Maimonides, it became clear to him in a way that it had never been before. His hand extended on its own and opened the book of Rabbi Akiva Eiger's glosses to see what innovations he had discovered about the passage, then he glanced at *The Expositions on the Book of Education* under the entry on the mitzvah *Shema*. The works of the Ancients and the Moderns appeared before him and their arguments pleased him, and he rejoiced in the Torah as he had never rejoiced in all his days. Suddenly he saw before him, shining and bright, the many insights he had had and the many passages he had explained throughout all those years.

The morning star had nearly risen before he dozed off. Upon falling asleep he dreamt. He saw a wrinkled piece of paper falling out of the pages of the Talmud. He unfolded it and, behold, there written in ornamental letters was: *Illumine our eyes in Thy Torah.* He interpreted it as a reference to himself: *Illumine our eyes in Thy Torah,* illumine my eyes that were blinded by Thy shining Torah. A ray of light streamed through the window and woke him. He rose with alacrity, washed his hands and recited the morning blessings. When he reached the blessings for the Torah and said, *O Lord our God! We beseech Thee, make pleasant the words of Thy Torah in our mouths,* he savored the sweetness he had tasted when reciting the psalms and studying the Mishnah. He continued the blessing: *so that we and our descendants and the descendants of Thy people, the house of Israel, may all know Thy name and study Thy Torah for its own sake.* He focused his attention: *for its own sake.*

From that day on Reb Moishe Dovid began his daily regimen with Psalms. As soon as he arrived in the house of study and took his seat, even before he opened a volume of the Talmud, he took the psalter and recited aloud the daily hymns in the same sweet melody he had sung the one night he felt his heart open to the Torah. Afterwards, when he plunged into the depths of a Talmudic passage, he tasted its pleasure anew and was filled with zeal and love. It seemed to him as if the wellsprings of wisdom had opened up before him: the meaning of the passage would become clear to him, and insights into the Torah would appear to him of their own accord. The friends who witnessed him chanting psalms in the house of study in such a common tune could not understand what had happened to him, but shook their heads and glanced at one another. Some whispered that he was praying for someone dangerously ill, others that he had been ensnared by the Hasidim.

After that incident, Reb Moishe Dovid sought to apologize to Ezra Siman Tov. He said to himself, I caused him anguish about the Rabbenu Tam tefillin in the Zoharei Hamah Synagogue, and again about the psalms in the Ahdut Yisrael Synagogue. When shall I make amends to this innocent man? He tried to do so, but was unsuccessful. Several years on the eve of the Day of Atonement he resolved to approach him, but each year he deferred it for one reason or another. Several times he saw him from a distance and made up his mind to approach him and make amends then and there, but before he finished deliberating on what to say and how to say it, Ezra had already disappeared. Every Friday Reb Moishe Dovid went to the elderly bookseller to examine both the new and old books. Each time he saw a copy of the Psalms he found attractive, he would say to himself, this is for Ezra. One time the bookseller showed him a spectacular edition of Psalms, bound in leather with letters in gold leaf, on white pages with perfect, pleasant, and shining letters, together with supplications for all possible moments, incantations from Haim Yosef David Azulai, the traveler's prayer, prayers for the mortally ill and explanations of the difficult words. He bought it on the spot. He opened the first page and inscribed in it: For Ezra Siman Tov. *Mark the innocent man, and behold the upright: for the end of that man is peace.*

Chapter twelve

In which we leave the reconciliation to its proper time, and recount the terrible story that Ezra told the writer about what happened fifty years ago on HaNevi'im Street.

One night after the evening prayer Ezra saw the writer pacing pensively in the synagogue courtyard. "O writer! O writer!" Ezra called out after him. The writer turned, his eyes beaming, and asked Ezra, "Have you heard any new tales?"

"I have a tale I should like to recount to you," said Ezra. "Whether it is new or old I do not know. Some tales seem new but are actually quite old; others are old but renew themselves daily. It happened fifty years ago, but to me it is new every day. Not a day passes that it does not recur before my eyes, and each time it appears to me in a different light.

"Fifty years ago we used to play in the field on HaNevi'im Street. Do you remember the field that was next to the school building, a place where the neighborhood children loved to play? At the time we were four boys. Yehudah Tawil, the professor, Moishe Dovid, the *avrech*, Rahamim Kalifa, the musician, and I. Almost every single day we went there to play. We were all neighbors and friends. One day after the sun had already set and the daylight was growing dim, we were engrossed in our game, screaming and shouting the way children do. A high wall bordered the field. Actually it was not so high, but in those days it seemed very high. At the foot of the wall lay piles of junk and nearby stood an old olive tree that had never borne any fruit. We had no idea what was behind the wall. Some said there was a monastery with nuns in black robes, others a hospital for the dangerously ill or even a leper colony. Various other rumors abounded. We had never seen anything with our own eyes. Not a single sound had ever emerged from there. No one went in and no one went out. There were children who recounted strange stories about what went on there. Once or twice I imagined I had seen a sort of black robe passing through, but I do not know if it actually happened."

Ezra's voice trembled.

"And then, sir, the ball we were playing with suddenly bounced over the wall. A ball, children, you know, the ball bounced, it bounced, this is what happens with a ball. 'Jump Rahamim,' Moishe Dovid called out. 'Yeah, jump Rahamim,' shouted Yehudah Tawil, 'come on, jump already, Ezra, what are you afraid of?' he called after us in a taunting voice. In truth, I was afraid. The two of us jumped over the wall, Rahamim and I. And then, what happened then? Sir, you are a writer, what happened? I heard a great crashing sound of cans and saw a huge cloud of dust, and I remember Rahamim's bitter cry, even today I still hear it ringing through my ears. And then Moishe Dovid screamed, 'Ezra, what have you done? What have you done?' But I do not remember having done a thing. 'How could you do such a thing?' Yehudah shouted at me, 'Ezra, Ezra, what have you done?' We all fled. This is all that I know. But every day the cloud of dust appears to me in another form, and Rahamim's cry in a different voice. What happened? Sir, you are a writer. What happened? What did I do?"

Ezra continued:

"Five years after that incident Rahamim's eyes grew dim. The doctors told him they had no remedy. I never asked him what happened to his eyes. What did I do, sir, you are a writer, did I commit a grave sin? What did I do? For fifty years not a single one of us has ever discussed what happened. Not with each other nor with anyone else. Not Yehudah Tawil, nor Moishe Dovid, nor Rahamim. No one asked and no one told. Even I did not ask. Except once, ten years ago, Moishe Dovid asked me if I knew how Rahamim grew sick. No, I have no idea, I said to him, and he stared at me with a peculiar expression. Over the years it seemed as if I had forgotten the matter, but every day, at prayer, my eyes fill with tears of their own accord. Several times when difficult things have happened to me I have calmly accepted my afflictions and said to myself, 'The creditor has found an opportunity to collect his debt.' When the great tragedy happened with my daughter, that same tragedy that shook all of Jerusalem, I justified the judgment to myself and said, my daughter, the apple of my eye. An eye for an eye.

"Several times when I have visited Rahamim, I have thought, now I will ask him how he got sick, why his eyes grew dim, but each time something prevents me and I do not ask. Why have I not asked, sir? Why? He has never told me of his own accord. He only asks me to recount tales to him. I recount a tale and he plays his violin. What did I do, sir? You are a writer. What happened there? What happened to Rahamim? Why did he go blind? You write stories. Please, write about what happened there. You are a writer and you write what comes to mind, and whatever you write will be what happened, what difference does it make to you, is that not so, sir? Is it not so?"

The writer was silent, pressed Ezra's hand with a blank expression, and went on his way.

Chapter thirteen

In which we leave Ezra in his bewilderment
and recount what befell him and Rahamim
the Blind at the feast held to celebrate
Ezra's escape from the divine punishment of
premature death.

Birthdays were not celebrated in Ezra's household. Not his,
nor his children's, and certainly not his wife's. It had not been done in
Ezra's father's house, and Ezra never did what had not been done in
his father's house. In general, the pure-minded of Jerusalem were not
accustomed to convene voluntary celebrations. If you saw the Jerusalem faithful preparing a banquet, it was most certainly a ritual meal;
either a circumcision feast, presided over by the Divine Presence, at
which the covenant between man and God is forged and both parties
of the covenant must be present; or a feast for the redemption of the
first-born son, which all the residents of Jerusalem hasten to attend,
for masters of the hidden knowledge say that he who participates in
such a feast merits the equivalent of eighty-four days of fasting, and

according to the mystical tradition it repairs known sins; or a feast of seven benedictions for the bride and groom, for he who brings joy to the newlywed is like one who rebuilds the ruins of Jerusalem; or a feast to mark the completion of a tractate from the Talmud, which according to the rabbis is celebrated as a holiday for scholars. But for the pure-minded of Jerusalem to prepare a celebration just like that, feasting upon meat and wine and listening to live music—such an affair was unheard of in Jerusalem. In the house of Ezra Siman Tov's father, when they used to hear that one of the new residents of Jerusalem had held a birthday party they would snicker and say: The only birthday mentioned in scripture is the wicked Pharaoh's. Still, when Ezra reached sixty years of age, his children and loved ones thought to make a party in his honor. He was against it. They pleaded with him unrelentingly but he did not want it, until he saw his children and loved ones begin to despair, and because he never insisted upon anything or refused to accommodate his friends, he shook his head in acquiescence and conceded begrudgingly. But there was another concealed reason he acceded to their desire: he had once heard from Haham Pinto that the sages of Baghdad said that one who reaches sixty years of age should hold a feast of thanksgiving, to praise and exalt the blessed Name for having escaped the divine punishment of premature death.

Although he had consented, his wife, Madame Sarah, was very wary of such a celebration and wanted to cancel it. On more than one occasion she appealed to him. Even though she did not reveal her fears to him, he intuitively understood her dread of the evil eye. Crowds of people would come and congratulate him on reaching old age in good health. "Why do we need such trouble?" she said. "We are settled in our own house, we conduct our lives in peace and quiet, and thank God there is no breach and no outcry. Why should we alter our ways? We have never conducted ourselves in such a manner, and certainly not in public. Who knows who will come, what will be said, or what will happen?" Although in his heart Ezra agreed with her, he assured her that she needn't have such vain fears, that the evil eye no longer held sway in those times. It is impossible to say that her fears were assuaged, but she, who never said a thing contrary to her husband, was silent. Had she known the celebration was against his will, that they had pleaded with him time after time, that he had begged them to leave him alone, she never would have yielded. But now, thinking it was his wish, she was silent, accepted it, and began to prepare the feast in the Aleppo tradition.

The children of Aleppo were proud of their ritual feasts, and they boasted of their distinctiveness. Their poets worked wonders in composing hymns pleasing to the soul, their cantors astounded all with melodies agreeable to the ear, their sages invented new interpretations of the Torah that sharpened the mind, their preachers recited parables that quickened the heart, their moralists delivered fiery orations that shook the soul, their women painstakingly prepared dishes pleasing to the palate, and even the remaining people who sat at the table, who were not scholars or preachers or poets or cantors, did not sit idly with their heads buried in their plates, but posed questions, ventured responses, exchanged banter, offered praise, poured scorn, hummed melodies, gestured with their hands, and winked at one another. This homily is very pleasing, they might say about one, but about another they would twist the corner of their mouths as if to say: we have already heard better. And when the cantor sang the scale with the appropriate flourish they would wave their hands as if to indicate the name of the scale, to show that they too were well versed in cantillation and not ignoramuses.

But woe to the poet who was not careful to preserve meter or rhyme, and woe to the cantor who confounded the scales, or the scholar who forgot even a single word from a biblical verse, or the preacher who delivered a homily he had already given, even many years earlier, and woe to the woman who packed the stuffing in the squash too tight, or if the grains of rice that she had cooked clumped together on the serving platter. Each and every ritual feast was so thoroughly prepared that it was as pleasing as could be, and even those of the poor were like the banquets of a king.

Some adorn their tables with flowers and blossoms, others with finely painted china, but the Jews of Aleppo crowned theirs with words of Torah, with hymns, and discussions of scholarship, for this was their beauty, so that a guest at their table who did not come from Aleppo, even a scholar in his own native land, stood in awe and feared to utter even the slightest word, and could not move before paying tribute: Blessed are you, O people of Aleppo, and blessed are your tables, for you are all scholars, from the least to the greatest.

At ritual feasts like these the Jews of Aleppo perform the *Brendizi*. What is a *Brendizi*? After the eating and drinking, when their hearts are full of the words of Torah and the parables of the wise, and their spirits are cheerful from the hymns, their glasses are filled with Arak and one of the guests raises his glass and calls out: *Ana ashrab hatha al-cas* (I shall drink this glass). Immediately everyone falls silent, and then calls out in response: *Ana ashrab hatha al-cas, Ana ashrab hatha al-cas*. All eyes fall upon him, and he stands up, spontaneously reciting in verse, opening with praise for the Lord, may He be blessed, composing poems in honor of joy, in tribute to the day itself, until he reaches the closing verse saying: I drink this glass in honor of so-and-so. Sometimes he composes verses in honor of the host, sometimes in honor of the hostess, or his own wife, or one of the guests whom he is particularly fond of. The *Brendizi* has no established limit, but depends on the abilities of the poet, the strength of the liquor, and the number of glasses he has drunk. The lesser among the guests rhyme for only four lines before reaching the closing verse, the ordinary reach as far as ten lines, and the truly extraordinary continue to rhyme without limit. But how does one judge a *Brendizi*? Not simply by the number of lines but by the precision of the rhyme, respect for the meter, and correctness of the grammar, for if the speaker does not adhere to the meter or the rhyme, the guests cry out mockingly, 'Focus!' But the poem is also evaluated for the element of surprise, that is to say, that the guests cannot guess the closing verse before it is uttered, and for its sharpness, erudition, and measure of humor. Whoever receives a *Brendizi* in his honor has to raise his glass and respond with his own. The best *Brendizi* composers arrange their verses in honor of their addressee, skillfully weave in allusions to the sayings of the sages and the hymns of the ancient poets, all to increase the joy and happiness of the occasion.

Many used to compose verses for the *Brendizi*, but no one could compare to Haham Tawil, the father of Doctor Yehudah. When Haham Tawil raised his glass and said *Ana ashrab hatha al-cas*, everyone would fall silent, gazing at him in anticipation of his poem, and he would look back at the crowd, alluding to a different guest with each and every rhyme, mentioning their deeds, until he had included them all in the beautiful garland of his poem. Woe to the one who interrupted his performance, for immediately he would turn his verses upon him, scathing him with his sharp tongue; at times he finished a line of his poem with a sound that not a single one of us could use in a rhyme scheme, or at best for only two or three lines, but he would maintain the rhyme for over fifteen lines without pausing to think for a moment. Everyone wondered where his great ability came from, or from what well he drew his words, but he responded modestly: it's the exceptional Arak, not me.

For many years Haham Tawil composed a *Brendizi* at each ritual feast, until at one feast an incident occurred. He began to compose a *Brendizi* as usual, when all of a sudden a verse eluded him. The guests were bewildered. He lowered his gaze, struggling to remember the verse, before giving up and gesturing to the wine-steward, as if to say, today's Arak differs from yesterday's. At the next feast he ignored the meter, and yet another time he forgot the closing verse. Everyone was astonished at what had happened to him, and bowed their heads to avoid embarrassing him. After it had occurred once, and then repeated itself, they hinted to one another: old age has caught up with him. For the *Brendizi*, because it was spontaneous and entirely oral, required agility, recall, and erudition, which are all weakened by old age. The sages said: scholars in their old age, the older they grow, the greater their peace of mind; peace of mind, perhaps, but their wit undoubtedly dulls. Such is the way of the world: at first people are silent out of respect; next they insinuate quietly; finally they speak about it openly. Haham Tawil began to decline until he had nearly stopped reciting the *Brendizi* altogether.

Once, I sat next to him at a ritual feast, and he revealed his secret to me. Turning to me, he opened: "Undoubtedly you are wondering about the *Brendizi* I used to compose, why people used to praise me and now they whisper to each other that I have stopped reciting them. Do you actually think I can't hear them murmuring to each other? Know, my son, it is not so. Know, that when my poems were so extraordinary, they did not praise my great cleverness; and now, when they mutter, it is not about my old age." He was silent for a few moments before continuing:

"Once, in my youth, I raised my glass to recite the *Brendizi*, and, beginning to recite the verses, I suddenly thought of a stinging remark about one of the guests to use as my closing verse, but one that would have given a mortal wound had I said it. With the glass in my hand, stringing one verse after another, I fought a battle with myself: If I said it, I would shame him in public; if I resisted the temptation, I would leave my brilliant remark unsaid. Thus I hesitated, telling myself, why not say it, I can appease him afterwards with another verse, and then, take control of yourself, don't embarrass another Jew in public. Throughout this struggle I continued to declaim verses of no particular importance, while everyone stared at me waiting to hear the closing verse. Finally, my good will got the better of me. Swallowing the closing verse I had wanted to declaim, I closed the poem on a banal note. Taken aback by the closing lines, everyone shouted at me in scorn: 'Focus, focus!' I was ashamed. But I said to myself, better I should be embarrassed than someone else.

"From that day on, whenever I raised my glass the rhyming verses simply flowed from my mouth, but I had no idea of their source. I felt as if I dreamt them; they were always beautiful, the closing verse leapt into my mouth of its own accord, everyone praised me. They thought it was all my own invention. This continued for many years. On one occasion, at a feast for the reading of the *Zohar*, they were selling the platter of Elijah the Prophet, the tray encircled with candles, to the one who would give most generously to charity, because it is considered particularly meritorious to acquire it. One of those present, who carried himself with great haughtiness, thought it would serve as a charm to ensure the marriage of his daughter, and had acquired it after outbidding all of his competitors with a very large sum. At that moment, an acerbic *Brendizi* about him occurred to me. Hastily raising my glass before my good will could take over, I slighted him in front of everyone. They all erupted in peals of laughter, and so he too feigned a smile of amusement, but I could see he was terribly offended. Although I sought to appease him with several other *Brendizi* poems, I knew he was not mollified. From that feast on, every time I raised my glass to recite a *Brendizi*, ready for the rhymed verses to roll off my tongue, I would forget a line, and could not understand why. As for the rest of the story, well, you already know it. As the days wore on, I kept forgetting the rhymes until I stopped reciting the *Brendizi*, and everyone assumed I had grown old. If the day comes when I manage to recite once again, then I will know that the man I offended has been reconciled and my sin has been wiped away. I wait for it every day."

From the moment they decided to hold the feast, Ezra's entire house was astir. Madame Sarah labored in preparation of the meal, assisted by her neighbors, who all peeled, stuffed, cooked, and baked by her side, while the children struggled to ensure they invited all Ezra's loved ones to the banquet. Every person who received an invitation responded joyfully, for they all loved Ezra and sought to honor him but had always lacked the opportunity. Even the writer was invited, but he never responded to the invitation.

When the day of his sixtieth birthday arrived, Ezra Siman Tov observed a private fast he had taken upon himself a few days earlier, and implored God during the afternoon prayer not to harm him because of the feast. With tears in his eyes, he said, "Master of the Universe, You know the secrets of the heart, it is obvious and known to You that I did not want this feast for my honor or for the honor of my family, but what could I do, ever since I have reached the age of discretion I have never defied my loved ones and I am unable to refuse those who plead with me. I could not bear to witness their suffering. May it be Your will that this feast be conducted decently, that there should be no mishap or impediment, and that it be for the honor of heaven."

All Ezra Siman Tov's relatives, friends, and associates gathered at the feast: Yehezkel Kaduri, the owner of the laundry; Raful Laniado, who sat next to him in the Zoharei Hamah Synagogue; Shaul Shem-tob, Yitzhak Barsano, Ya'akob Tzadkah, and Yitzhak Aminof, his friends who studied the *Hok L'Yisrael* with him every morning; Reb Zev Wolf, Reb Haim Mikhul, and Reb Abraham Yitzhak, from the Zikhron Kedoshim Synagogue; Nahum Ashrof and Michael Ben-tov, the beadles of the Ahdut Israel Synagogue; Mahlof Alfasi, the spice vendor from the Mahane Yehudah market; and many others. Even the scholars, who do not attend feasts unless they know who else will attend, came to this one: Haham Mas'oud Baghdadi, the professional scribe from Malachi Street; Haham Zion Ventura, the homilist, dubbed thus because of the many parables he included in his Sabbath sermons; Haham Kahanof, who taught *The Ben Ish Hai*; and the greatest of them all, the great rabbi, Haham Yosef Pinto. His two childhood friends came as well; his great brother-in-law, Doctor Yehudah Tawil, and Reb Moishe Dovid. Even the uninvited were not particular fussy; they swallowed their pride, and turned up to show their great love for him.

After having cleared Ezra's house of all its furniture and bring-ing in the great long table from the synagogue, Ezra, his family, his wife's family, the members of the synagogue, the scholars, and the guests all seated themselves at the table with a volume of the sacred *Zohar* open before them, and read from the chapter beginning *Abraham was now old, advanced in years, and the Lord blessed Abraham in all things.* Each one read a paragraph aloud, for the reading of the *Zohar* is a benefit to the pure soul, even one who cannot understand it. They partook of the delicacies on the table and sang melodies. After several songs, they brought out a bottle of wine and recited the bless-ing for the wine. They finished it and brought in another, an even better bottle, and called upon Ezra Siman Tov to make the blessing of *the good and Him who causes all good,* to focus on all the blessings he had received from the One who rewards all living beings. Finally, they poured glasses for all the guests, and Raful Laniado raised his and said: *Ana ashrab hatha al-cas.* Immediately everyone fell silent and turned towards him, and he looked at Ezra and Madame Sarah:

> *Better than a distant brother is a neighbor near,*
> *He who has found a wife has found what's dear,*
> *For Madame Sarah and Ezra Siman Tov I drink this beer!*

Saul Shemtob in turn raised his glass:

> *Wisdom in old age, knowledge at its peak,*
> *In honor of our host, we are not silent but speak,*
> *I drink this glass for Ezra who has gone grey,*
> *For those who at Zikhron Kedoshim pray!*

Everyone looked intently at the Ashkenazim from Zikhron Kedoshim to see if they would respond. They were unacquainted with this custom and did not know what to do. But when Zev Wolf realized that everyone was waiting for their response, he raised his glass:

> *We of the Ashkenazi congregation*
> *Unfamiliar with Zohar or versification*
> *Unlearned in rhyme evaluation*
> *Yet boldly we turn to the exaltation*
> *Of our Ezra, precious beyond computation*

Thus they continued to compose poems celebrating the guest of honor, Madame Sarah, the feast itself, and the scholars.

It could not be said that they reached the heights of poetry, but they certainly brought happiness. Doctor Tawil, occupied throughout with the editing of his great article, which he held on his lap, would occasionally lift his head and turn his attention to the would-be poets. Once he could not restrain himself and turned to his friend

Reb Moishe Dovid, who was sitting next to him, buried in a book of Talmudic glosses, "This is what they call *Brendizi*? Better that they should remain silent. Can any of them compare with my honorable father, the crown upon our heads, who would raise his glass and recite eighteen verses in perfect rhyme, a line for each and every one of the guests, return to the guest of honor and his wife with the closing verse, and fill the entire poem with allusions to Scripture, Mishnah and Talmud?"

They returned to the songbooks, and the cantors embellished the melodies they had introduced earlier. After several songs the beadles of Ahdut Yisrael Synagogue brought out the prayer books for the Day of Atonement and put them down in front of the guests, while Doctor Tawil brought out his great volume of the sacred hymns of Abraham Ibn Ezra, published by the Israeli Academy of Sciences, and they began to sing the hymn *Son of the Land*, which includes an account of man's entire life, with the melody used by the Jews of Aleppo immediately following the evening prayer on the Day of Atonement. The rest sang with the prayer books printed and published by Salah Mansour, but Doctor Tawil carefully scrutinized the great book of the university with its introductions, footnotes, and sources.

They all sang the hymn:

> *O son of Adam, call to mind thy birth,*
> *And at thy death return thee to the earth.*

And each one in turn read a stanza aloud. Yehezkel Kaduri began:

> *Rise up! – so says one to a boy of five –*
> *and scale the rocky heights 'mid rugged boulders,*
> *while still he draws from mother's milk his life*
> *and rides aloft upon his father's shoulders.*

Ya'akob Tzadkah:

> *Hasten not to rebuke a lad of ten*

As yet so young, too soon by life chastised:
Speak tender loving words to him, for then
By family and friends he will be prized.

Shaul Barsano:

Behold how lustily a youth of twenty
Skips over mountains like a nimble fawn,
With beauty – such a lethal trap – in plenty,
But for his teacher's anger only scorn.

Shaul Shemtob:

Willy-nilly upon forty he stumbles
Bad or good—to his fate resigned
Hurrying, to friends he only mumbles,
His affairs, his work ever on the mind.

Yitzhak Aminof, who had recently turned fifty, was honored with the next stanza:

At fifty he recalls his wasteful days
Grieving as times of mourning hasten near,
Contemptuous of the world and all its ways:
'My time has come' he mutters now in fear.

After each recitation they all repeated the chorus:

O son of Adam, call to mind thy birth,
And at thy death return thee to the earth.

When they reached the stanza for age sixty, all fell silent and turned toward Ezra. He read in a trembling voice:

At sixty, 'What', you ask, 'is now his fate?'

He hurries on to action and achievement:
His feeble limbs can only contemplate,
They cannot stir to yet another movement.

If threescore years and ten his span may reach
His doings are no longer heard or seen:
His former friends ignore his every speech
they see him as a burden, vile and mean.

A weight at eighty on his family –
His mind, his eyes have both now given up:
To all around a foolish mockery,
With wormwood on his plate, gall in his cup.

Beyond this, he is reckoned to be dead:
Happy is he who will a sojourner befriend;
His mind has long since taken to its bed,
He ponders only his reward and end.

As he read line after line, his mind flooded with thoughts. Scenes from his life passed before his eyes out of all sequential order; experiences he had had as an adult, as a young man, but again and again the doubt plagued his heart, of whether he had been forgiven for that sin. Across from him sat Yehezkel Kaduri, his glass in his hand, nodding towards him with his head. Now he imagined himself in Yehezkel Kaduri's laundry. How many years had he worked for him, day after day, hour after hour, with the shirt in his hand, he labored and toiled to rid it of the stain, his cheeks reddened, as the dust emitted by the clothing sullied his eyes. *O son of Adam, call to mind thy birth, And at thy death return thee to the earth.* And what did he have to show for it? *My youthful vigor cares but for itself. When will I my haughty spirit save?*

The beadle from the Zoharei Hamah Synagogue tapped his fork on the glass in his hand as if he had something to say. As a silence fell over the room, he invited Haham Pinto to deliver his homily.

Haham Pinto opened with a citation from scripture: "*The innocence of the upright will guide them.* It is said: Mark the innocent man, and behold the upright: for the end of that man is peace. The Torah says, *Thou shalt be innocent with the Lord thy God*; and it says, *Walk before me and be thou innocent.* We know that Scripture praises our forefather Jacob: But Jacob was *an innocent man, dwelling in tents.* On the face of it, what is so exalted about innocence? Rashi explains: one who is not shrewd in deception is called innocent. But take heed! It is not written, one who is not shrewd, but rather one who is not shrewd in deception is called innocent. People think that the innocent man is one who is not shrewd, but they are mistaken. In fact, it takes great effort for one who is shrewd to conduct himself innocently in his affairs. Scripture says, *The Lord preserves man and beast* and the sages interpreted this to mean those who, though cunning in their judgment, place themselves as a beast before the Lord. One who is not cunning, what praise does he deserve for conducting himself in innocence? But one who possesses a subtle and expansive mind, and nevertheless walks before the Lord in innocence; appeals to him in repentance as a son before his father; deigns not to consult sorcery or attempt to determine the future, but directs his mind to trust in God; seeks the Lord; is content with his lot; loves the Lord as well as his fellow man; strives to bring happiness both to his Maker and to other people; one whose affairs and actions are neither crooked nor perverse—it is this man whom Scripture praises. A story is told about a prince, the son of a king, who descended from his chariot to pursue a deer in the hunt. Chasing after it as it fled from him, he ran through the forest until he finally gave up. And he found himself all alone, wandering in the woods, seeking his way, calling and crying for his father, but no one could hear him, the sun had set, the day had darkened, and hearing the cries of wild animals, he grew frightened of them, and of bandits. What did he do?"

Thus Haham Pinto recounted the fable and its moral, the acrostic and numerology. He said to them: "E, Z, R, A. The Hebrew letter for E equals seventy when one counts letters as numerals, Z equals seven, which gives us seventy-seven, R in numerology equals two hundred, which gives two hundred seventy-seven," and all the guests counted on their fingers to verify his sum, "A in numerology equals one—this gives us two hundred seventy-eight. SIMAN TOV is another one hundred seventy-seven, for a total of..."

At this point, all of them lost track of the computation and nodded their heads in agreement to indicate their trust in him, all except for two: Doctor Tawil and Reb Moishe Dovid, who were testing the Haham to see if his calculation turned out to be correct; a total of four hundred and fifty five, and in numerology this equals the value of the phrase in Scripture, '*He is innocent.*' Computing the sum in his head, Doctor Tawil realized it did not add up and started to leap out of his chair to point out the mistake, but Haham Pinto had already anticipated his objection and turned to him:

"Fear not, sir, I know, I know the sum equals four hundred and fifty-two, but if you include one for each word—Ezra, Siman, Tov—the sum will work out."

They all looked at Doctor Tawil and smiled that their own Haham Pinto had triumphed over the professor. Haham Pinto concluded his homily: "This is the meaning of our verse: *The innocence of the upright will guide them.* In the end, those who act in innocence, it is their innocence that guides them in a righteous manner and illuminates their eyes."

Before Haham Pinto had even finished saying "illuminates their eyes," the door opened. Everyone turned towards it and saw the writer standing in the doorway. Silence descended upon the room. The writer surveyed all the guests in the room with one glance and entered maintaining a blank expression. As they continued to stare at the writer, they saw someone following him, standing erect, clutching at the writer's coat, a cane in one hand, a violin in the other, and his eyes sealed by his eyelids. A hush fell over the room, such that not even the faintest whisper could be heard. All eyes turned toward the man. In the entrance stood Rahamim Kalifa the musician. He lingered in the doorway like one waiting to see what would happen, raising his eyelid with his fingers, he then took hold of the table and sat down at its head. It just so happened that this seat was next to that of Ezra Siman Tov.

All the guests froze. One could not hear the slightest sound. Everyone knew Rahamim Kalifa had not left his house for many years. They waited for something momentous to occur but knew not what to expect. After several moments of enduring silence, Rahamim got to his feet, picked up his violin, tucked it under his chin, took his bow in his right hand and began to play. A moment later the room was filled with a melody the likes of which no ear had ever heard. The melody was unlike anything they recognized. It was unlike the melodies of the dawn hymns in the Ades Synagogue, or the tunes for the Sanctification prayer in the Mosayof Synagogue, or the songs sung by the Jews of Aleppo at their ritual feasts, or the hymns for the Days of Awe in the Salonika Synagogue, or the melodies used by the cantor in the Roman Synagogue. It had a trace of each one. Some of the hymn, some of the mystery, the sadness and the joy, all fused into one; and a fragment of holiness hovered over it. One by one they all closed their eyes, and each one imagined the melody addressed to him, telling him the story of his life.

Doctor Tawil closed the great book that he was perpetually examining and sat in astonishment, his eyes opened. He had never seen or heard anything like this, a man playing a simple fiddle that seemed to recount to him the story of his entire life, from the games of his childhood through his studies and research up to the meditations of his old age. He turned to ask Reb Moishe Dovid whether he felt the same thing but saw him sitting with his eyes closed, nodding toward Rahamim at each and every interval. Rahamim continued playing, his face looking like that of someone standing at prayer purifying himself before the Lord, and everyone in the room thought the prayer was on his own behalf. Haham Pinto whispered to those seated at his side that this was what the Levites must have sounded like in the Temple at the time of the sacrifices. At one moment the tune would seem about to end in hushed tones, only to burst forth in a mighty crescendo. But suddenly it stopped. As unexpectedly as it had begun, so it ceased. They all opened their eyes as if they were returning from far-off worlds and did not know what to say.

Rahamim got to his feet, as if he were looking at all the guests and said: "Gentleman, you all know that I never leave my own house. I was not even invited to this feast. You are certainly wondering why I have come here. But if you listen carefully to what I have to say, it will be clear to you that it was impossible for me not to be here."

Rahamim turned towards Ezra Siman Tov. Ezra's face blanched. Then Rahamim turned towards Reb Moishe Dovid and Doctor Tawil, who sat nervously with drawn faces.

"I shall recount to you a tale that happened fifty years ago. Four children were playing in a field."

All the guests fixed their gaze upon Rahamim. Ezra's face, already pale, grew even whiter. He looked at the writer, seeking to find some sort of clue in his expression. Had the writer not told him what the Baal Shem Tov had said: when the day comes and you hear your own story from someone else, know that your remedy has come? He imagined that he detected a faint flicker in the writer's eyes, as well as a thin smile, as if to say, I have already written the conclusion to this tale, but immediately after the thought occurred to him, the writer's face went blank again. Doctor Tawil rested his head on his palms, and Reb Moishe Dovid fixed his gaze upon the empty space in the room. The writer took out a small notepad and a pencil and began to scribble notes.

"Four children," Rahamim continued, "were playing together in the field next to the Talmud Torah on HaNevi'im Street. There was a high wall, very high, and the children were enjoying their ballgame. The sun was setting and the day had begun to fade, they had nearly finished their game, when the ball bounced over the wall next to the old olive tree that had never borne fruit. We were four children. I was one of them. We did not know what was on the other side of the wall. We had heard many things. Two of us climbed the wall. 'Jump,' called out one of the other boys. 'Jump,' a second one said to me, 'what's a coward like you afraid of?' I was scared to jump, but I dreaded their ridicule even more. I jumped. There was a great noise. A big cloud."

Ezra's eyes began to shed tears. Rahamim continued to tell the story. Silence filled the room. "My eyes dimmed," Rahamim said, "light began to flash before me like lightning filled with many black dots. I had nearly fallen into a pit and into a flaming fire. I thought to myself, I am lost. I let out a great shriek, and I heard noises. I was afraid of the fire, but even more afraid that people would come from the great building beyond the wall, take me away, and shut me up forever behind the green metal doors. But then one of the other boys jumped down and extended a hand to me. What a wonderful hand. He pulled me up behind him. He saved my life. That boy is here right now, with you, sitting at the table. That boy is Ezra Siman Tov."

Everyone turned and stared at Ezra. His face was drenched with tears. Slowly his color was returning and his eyes brightening. The entire time, he had been crying and looking at the storyteller. Rahamim continued.

"We all fled in fear. Not a soul heard what happened. Even amongst ourselves we did not speak about it. From time to time, my eyes hurt, especially when they were struck by strong winds, but I continued to live my regular life and was not concerned about anything. Several years later, the pain grew worse. I went to doctors, and tried various remedies. After years of seeking assorted medical treatments the doctors told me there was no hope. With each passing day, I saw less and less. There was not a single doctor in all Jerusalem who I did not visit. Until one day my world went totally dark. Black bitterness swept over me. Every day, before I began the morning prayers, I would take my fingers and raise my right eyelid to see if the day had brightened for me, and I thought I saw a bit of light, but I was probably imagining things. I shut myself up in a room, with my 'oud and occasionally my violin. When I would pick up my violin and play, I imagined my eyes were open and that I could see the world in all its glory; the world filled with different colors. With my violin I would pray and implore, with it I would hope and anticipate, but sometimes in the middle of the melody I would see that wall again, and hear that noise, and the melody would descend to the very depths, getting darker and darker. But then a ·

ray of white light would ascend like the dawning of the day and the melody would soar and shine, soar and shine, until it nearly brought joy to my soul. Thus many years passed. And then, after fifty years, another incident occurred that changed my life.

"Several months ago, the doctors informed me that a famous professor of ophthalmology was coming to Jerusalem from Canada, an expert in my particular illness, a man with a worldwide reputation, who had made many great discoveries and received numerous honors. They said that in the last year he had discovered something new in the treatment of my disease, and although they did not believe he could help heal my eyes, because my eye muscles had already deteriorated from not having been exposed to light for so many years, they agreed to refer me to him if I so desired. If it couldn't help, it certainly couldn't hurt. Yet I should not deceive myself, they said.

"If I so desired, they said. If I so desired? Is there anything I wanted more than this? I grew agitated and excited. During those days, every time I took up my violin it performed of its own accord and played happier and happier melodies, until I felt I needed to stop playing the violin and I began to petition with my lips. Only on Thursday evenings, when Ezra Siman Tov came to visit me, did I take up my violin. I did not tell a single soul, lest I be proven wrong and the object of their ridicule; I kept all my hope locked in my heart. Not even to Ezra, who is dearer to me than my own soul, did I suggest anything, and he continued, as he had for so many years, to listen to the melodies of my violin and recount stories to me. But his stories were filled with more and more light and more and more hope. My violin heard Ezra's stories and its melody ascended higher and higher, opening new horizons for me.

"Several months ago the professor arrived. I waited on a long line until he received me. He examined me and said five words: there might be a chance. Pausing for a moment, he said that a recently invented operation might be able to save one of my eyes, the right one, apparently because it had been exposed to a bit of light every day, but that the procedure was dangerous and he would only undertake it as a last resort. In my situation, it was probably the advisable treatment.

He would give me a bit of time to think it over before coming to a decision and informing him. I said to him then and there, 'I don't need any time and I don't need to think anything over, you are a messenger of the Almighty, do whatever you can and the rest is up to Heaven, please, make an appointment for me.' He fixed a date.

"What has happened to me from that day until today I cannot recount to you or anyone else. What I saw in my dreams, what I felt while I was awake, my petitions, my tears, the melodies I played. Only a single melody am I able to play from those days—I remember every single note, for it was carved into the deepest recesses of my heart—the melody I played for you today. I will never forget it as long as I live. I called it, *My soul, wait thou only upon God; for my expectation is from Him.* When Ezra heard it, he called it *The Dawning of the Day.* What I can tell you now is the end of the story. Several weeks ago the professor operated on me. Since then I have remained in total darkness. But he treated me every single day. A week ago at dawn they removed my bandage and I raised my eyelid."

The room was entirely silent. Not a sound was heard. All eyes were fixed upon Rahamim. Only Ezra kept his closed. The writer began writing furiously in his notebook, looking up and then writing, looking up and then writing. Rahamim continued:

"If all the seas were ink and all their reeds were quills, I could not describe that moment." He took up his violin and began to play. The melody was sweet and joyful. Without ceasing to play, he continued, "Light. White light appeared before me, like the morning star rising with light. I could see shadowlike images. With each passing hour it grew brighter and brighter. The professor asked me, 'What do you see?' 'Light,' I responded, 'Light.' 'Where can you see light?' he asked. Then clasping my hand, he said to me, 'We've done it.' It was well that he said it in the plural, for Heaven helped him.

"Suddenly countless doctors, each one wanting to attend to my eye and examine it with his lamp, surrounded us. I had no idea what was happening. If I had had my violin at the time, I would have begun to play. But I was in a hospital, and was at a loss for words. I was silent, and tears trickled down from my eyes. Different tears.

Not the same tears that had filled my life for more than forty years. The professor filled my hand with various medicines and entrusted me to the care of one of his assistants. With each passing day, I improved. Yesterday they sent me home. The doctors thought I was a family man and many people would certainly come to care for me, but actually not a soul knew what had happened to me. Today they allowed me to go out for a few hours. I had no idea where to go or what to do. As I was thinking about where to go, a man came to me and said he was a writer. Ezra had told me about him a couple of times. I couldn't understand why he suddenly appeared before me. I didn't know if he knew what had happened to me, and if so, where and how he had heard, or if he had no idea and appeared by coincidence. The writer did not explain a thing, he just asked me if I wanted him to accompany me to the feast they were making in honor of Ezra Siman Tov, who reached his sixtieth year and escaped spiritual excommunication. I came with him."

Rahamim fell silent and continued to play the violin. Suddenly he stopped. He looked at all of the guests seated around him and began to call out their names: "Our Rabbi, Haham Pinto, Doctor Yehudah Tawil, Reb Moishe Dovid," until he reached Ezra, and said: "Siman Tov. Ezra, Ezra Siman Tov." He went to him and fell on his neck.

"Rahamim," whispered Ezra as tears poured onto his face.

"Ezra, Ezra Siman Tov," Rahamim exclaimed.

A thought occurred to Ezra, but he could not grasp its nature. A meditation mingled with grief and sparks of happiness. The image of his daughter appeared before him. It had already been several years since he had last thought about her. He had always justified the judgment and said, "an eye for an eye." But now, as Rahamim fell on his neck, he imagined her too on his neck, looking at him with her innocent eyes and a faint smile on her lips, that same look she used to have when she sat on his lap after she came home from school. But then she disappeared. Ezra could not understand where the image had come from or where it had gone.

Chapter fourteen

In which we leave Ezra to his thoughts and recount what befell him in the laundry in Mahane Yehudah.

A few days later, as he was leaving the synagogue after the evening prayer, Ezra saw the writer. He asked him, "Ezra, have you no story?"

"Sir, you have just concluded the previous story and now you already want to hear a new one? Did you not write a pleasing conclusion to that one?" Ezra replied. The writer shook his head from side to side. Ezra was taken aback. "Is that not so, sir, O writer? Has the story not reached its conclusion?" As he asked, the concern was apparent in his voice. The writer shook his head again, indicating otherwise. "And what new episode have you to tell me?" Ezra asked.

"I have nothing to recount," replied the writer, "my legs carry me along, and I simply observe and record."

Ezra worried even more. He knew not why. The writer turned toward home. Ezra hurried after him. "If so, how will it end? What will be, sir, O writer? You most certainly know?"

The writer was silent. Ezra continued to accompany him along the way. Finally the writer turned to him and said, "Some are led by their hearts; others lead their hearts, and their end I cannot know. Some appear active and vigorous and yet are controlled by their destiny, others who are innocent and pure, appear to follow the events of their own lives but actually, in their purity, they become heroes who shape their own fortunes. How can I know?" The writer turned and hurried on his way.

Time passed and the days returned to their normal pace. Ezra went back to work. He was not fond of days filled with tension, for stress excites the heart, confuses the mind, and disturbs the equanimity of the soul. Ezra liked simple days, days when nothing seemed to happen, days that began with the regular morning service at dawn in the Zoharei Hamah Synagogue, continued with work at Kaduri's laundry and the market shopping in Mahane Yehudah, and concluded with Rabbi Kahanof's class on Jewish law in *The Ben Ish Hai*. Perhaps most of the world would consider such days dull, but for Ezra they were full of color.

In the morning he fixed his gaze upon the sunrise, and every morning it seemed to be a different shade. Every day he recited the same prayer, but each time he meditated on a different word that seemed new to him; as he reflected, it seemed as if he were dreaming, but the word brought before him the world and its fullness. When he arrived at the laundry for work, which was regular and unvarying, he found something new in it every time. In the morning he saw the owner Yehezkel in the same spot, but every day he appeared to wear a different expression on his face. He heard his greeting in the morning and farewell in the evening, and every day he perceived it another way. Every time he cleaned a prayer shawl of its stains he thought of a different image in his mind. One time the stain appeared to him as a sin which required cleansing, and as he scrubbed it, he prayed for the gates to be opened and for his repentance to be accepted, rising all the way to the heavenly throne; another time he imagined that a groom ascending to the Torah in the new prayer shawl given to him by his bride, his heart filled with joy and love, had discovered mud splattered upon it and worried that it foretold a bad omen; but Ezra cleaned the prayer shawl, smoothed it, and soothed it, and calmed the groom and his bride, and blessed them that they might establish a faithful household and that the Divine Presence might dwell in it. All Ezra's days were filled with colorful images.

One morning, when he arrived at the laundry, Ezra received Yehezkel Kaduri's usual greeting. It was the same greeting as any other day, but on this day Ezra thought he could hear an echo of pain. He looked into Yehezkel's eyes and detected a touch of concern. Ezra took a seat beside him and asked: "Yehezkel, what's the matter?" If anyone else had posed such a question Yehezkel would have merely dismissed him with a shrug of his shoulders, but not Ezra. He knew that he could not simply dismiss Ezra.

"There are rumors going round the market," answered Yehezkel. "I have heard the same report from several different people. The first to tell me was Prosper the tinman." Prosper Azulai was their neighbor at the laundry; he fixed Sabbath kettles and kerosene stoves. "According to what he heard, the city municipality wants to widen Jaffa Road near the market to construct a giant shopping center and to allow the buses to pass through more easily. They say several wealthy developers and several contractors have their eye on the area. Therefore, the municipality plans to close down a number of shops soon. They don't know which ones. Some claim they'll close all the shops from here to the plaza, others to Manny's Pharmacy; some say they will compensate us with money, others that they will just give us shops on Rashi Street or Meyuhas Street. People say famous lawyers are handling the affair, as well as real-estate appraisers. Presumably they'll take a huge percentage of the profit. I don't know what's going to happen, Ezra, I just don't know. Even without these troubles the income from the shop has declined over the last years; practically the only customers we have left are elderly, and several of them have gone to meet their maker. I don't know where young people have their prayer shawls cleaned these days. They say people will simply bury a stained prayer shawl and buy a new one. They have no emotional attachment to an old prayer shawl that has soaked up the tears of prayer, or no energy to deal with cleaning the stains. They prefer to replace them; they think the new ones are nicer than the old ones that we have cleaned. Maybe brides have stopped buying their grooms a prayer shawl for the bridal canopy and get them other things, and who knows how they are dressed when they ascend to the Torah? May the Merciful One have compassion. Even you and I, we are not as young as we once were. Do you think we can just relocate to another street and start over from the beginning? Where will I get the money to move the machines? Anyway, I'm worried that if I move them from their place, they will break. Once, when Prosper Azulai was greasing them, as he has for the last fifty years, he said to me that if anyone else besides him touches them, they will break down."

Ezra looked at Yehezkel and could see the anguish on his face. For fifty years they had been working together in the laundry. They were like brothers. When he was a young boy in Talmud Torah, a schoolboy who wanted to make a little money like all the other schoolboys in Jerusalem, he would help out in the afternoons, folding the prayer shawls that had been laundered at Kaduri's and observing the work. From time to time he even helped the workers. As the years went by, he learned the craft and impressed Yehezkel Kaduri and was eventually put in charge of the ironing. Ezra knew he had no words of comfort; that these rumors usually turned out to be true; that Yehezkel lacked the strength to transfer the laundry to another location; and how much pain it would cause him to close it. He did not want to offer meaningless consolations, so he said nothing; he just sat by Yehezkel's side and was silent. He had once heard from Haham Pinto that when friends sit together, even in silence there is a measure of comfort.

Several days later registered letters arrived by post to all the shops. A messenger asked them to sign for theirs. Yehezkel did not want to open it. Prosper came in and asked if they knew what was in the letter. Shemtob, who sold Turkish *borekas* with hard-boiled eggs and *sahlep* with cinnamon, also came in to ask. He had not signed. In general, he refused to sign anything. "No," replied Yehezkel, "no, I haven't opened it yet. We have a lot of work to do at the laundry just now and the customers are waiting, this isn't the time for reading reports."

That day, when Ezra returned home, Madame Sarah could see the pain on his face. He told her what was happening.

"Ezra," she said to him, "your entire life you have agonized that you don't spend enough time studying Torah. If what you are afraid of turns out to be true, you can spend more time studying Torah, for your time will be your own."

Ezra Siman Tov knew that what she said made sense, he had thought of this himself, but even so, her words did not enter his heart or soothe his pain. Such is the way of the world—a man always looks forward to a time when he will be free of his concerns and have the liberty to do the many things he has planned, but when the day comes and he suddenly has all the time in the world, he is dumbfounded and overwhelmed.

The rumor spread to the other workers in the laundry as well as the neighboring shops. Work continued by force of habit. They received clothing and returned it to the customers. But everything was different. Without the flavor of life. Everyone whispered quietly, as if someone were very ill. The happiness disappeared. All knew that their lots had been cast and their days numbered. Day after day the neighboring shop owners entered Kaduri's wearing worried looks. Some still held on to the hope that they could delay the inevitable through legal action. Several young lawyers encouraged them by saying they had a hope with this or that judge. A petty bureaucrat from one of the minor political parties went around saying he would speak to so-and-so, who was an important person with great influence on several other people who knew so-and-so, who had once worked in the municipality and sat on the committee in charge of the whole affair. Maybe they should think of giving him a little present for the festival. He also said that his party would not allow something like this to happen. In no way, shape, or form. He would see to it personally. So he said, as he stuffed himself with Shemtob's hot fresh *borekas* with hard-boiled eggs sprinkled with *za'atar*. He too knew that no one actually believed him. There were no newcomers around here.

But he had to say something. Sudri, the owner of the children's toy store, hung a great cord in front of his store and tied several bicycles to it, as well as a basket filled with multi-colored balls. He said he was going to put a big order of merchandise in for the coming festival of Purim. He refused to believe that anyone would widen the street and force him to close his shop. According to him, they were just rumors spread by some businessman who wanted to lower the real-estate prices and buy up all the shops. He had heard that someone had already done something similar in a big city and become very wealthy, and in the end it had turned out to be just rumors. But he said it with such distress that you could tell he didn't even believe it himself. Even Ezra's stories began to sound worn-out, and his parables lacked their usual lesson.

Thoughts troubled Ezra. The days felt longer than usual, and his work became wearisome, so as he scrubbed the garments with his hands he tried to cheer himself up with different images. He imagined himself in the morning, instead of going from his house to the laundry, turning toward the hall of study and sitting at the table, opening a volume of the Talmud and splitting hairs with scholars in the academy, they querying him about a point of Jewish law and he responding to them. He was sure that such thoughts would please him and could not understand why he was still dejected.

The weeks passed. Occasionally they saw surveyors setting up their equipment on the sidewalk and marking all kinds of different signs with little red stakes. In the beginning they stared at them as they did their work, trying to figure out what would happen. A little while later they stopped paying any attention. What difference did it make, they said, they would close it all up, it was already clear.

Chapter fifteen

In which we leave the surveyors to their red stakes and recount the passing of Haham Pinto.

One day as Ezra was reciting the morning prayers at dawn in the Zoharei Hamah Synagogue, he noticed that Haham Pinto had not arrived. Fear took hold of him. Haham Pinto had never once arrived late to morning prayers, not in the summer when the nights are short and the body weary, nor in the winter when the nights are cold and chill lures one to sleep. The Haham always rose early, with alacrity. Every day he noted the precise time of the appearance of light, the sun's rising, and the proper time for the wrapping of the prayer shawl. He went so far as to count his steps. From his house he went to the ritual bath and immediately afterwards to the synagogue. Thus it was every day. Neither snow nor rain, nor aches or pains, prevented him. Once he had recounted in jest: "Someone once asked me why I am so scrupulous to rise early every morning, and I replied, when my time comes to stand before the heavenly court, they will ask me if I duly fulfilled all the precepts. As I ready my response, they will probably bring the great code of law, the *Shulhan Aruch*, and inquire whether I have performed each and every article, and after all, the opening words of the *Shulhan Aruch* in article one, paragraph one are: *He shall rise up like a lion in the morning to worship his Creator who wakes the dawn.* Is it agreeable for someone to humiliate himself on the very first question?"

Throughout the opening psalms, until the cantor reached the Call to Prayer that marks the middle of the service, Ezra was waiting for Haham Pinto to arrive. When he saw that he had not arrived by the time they reached the Call to Prayer, he knew something had happened. Throughout the entire service he could not concentrate and his thoughts were confused. After the service, Haham Eliyahu Raful, HaMekhaven, pounded his hand on the reading desk and said: "We shall recite psalms for the recovery of our teacher, and call out his full name and the name of his mother." In a trembling voice he chanted the psalms appropriate for those who are gravely ill, and the entire congregation responded verse by verse.

The synagogue was filled with anguish and concern. Several members of the congregation suggested they perform a special *Tikkun Karet* to help the Haham's recovery, but the Haham's relatives indicated that he had issued specific instructions not to do anything on his behalf and not to alter any part of the synagogue service. They were not allowed to visit him, so as not to disturb his rest. Several days later they were informed that the situation had become quite grave and that Haham Pinto had requested their presence. Before they entered, the doctor warned them of the severity of his situation and asked them to choose their words carefully, lest they cause any unnecessary excitement, and told them to stay for only a few minutes. They entered.

Haham Pinto was lying on his bed, his face turned towards them. In a weak voice he said to them, "The doctor thinks I do not know what he knows, he asked you not to frighten me. I am not afraid of these moments. Someone who has spent his whole life learning to live truthfully does not fear death. No, I am not afraid of death, but I do fear what Yohanan Ben Zakkai feared. He responded to his students when they asked him why he was crying: If I were being taken before a king of flesh and blood, who is here today and in the grave tomorrow, whose greatest rage is ephemeral, whose punishment of me would not last forever, even if he put me to death, I could easily appease him with words and bribe him with money, and nevertheless, I would still be crying. But now, when I am being taken before the King of Kings, who reigns forever and ever, who if He is angry with me His anger is eternal, if He afflicts me His afflictions are perpetual, if He puts me to death, the death is everlasting, whom I cannot appease with words or bribe with money; and what is more, when I have before me but two paths, one to paradise, the other to Gehenna, and I know not which one I will be led down—shall I not cry? But still Rabbi Yohanan Ben Zakkai said he sang before the King. What shall I respond after him?" Tears filled his eyes. He added, "Know that even in these moments my faith in the Lord has not faltered, but because man knows not when his time will come, and the sages said that one who takes to his bed should think of himself as before the gallows. I want to issue several instructions to you."

He uttered words of rebuke and concluded, "My brothers, my friends, I beseech you, let there be always love and fellowship among you, peace and friendship, do not allow the demon of dissent to divide you; it has already dispersed several communities and destroyed several synagogues. Be like the sons of Aaron, lovers of peace, pursuers of peace, lovers of your fellow men, bringing them closer to the Torah."

A flicker of a smile appeared on his face and he said, "And now, I would like you to recite together with me the hymn *To thee my Lord, my yearning*, with the melody we sing every year in the evening service of the Day of Atonement before *Kol Nidre*, for it contains words of contrition and longing."

Silence took hold. No one uttered a word. The Haham intimated that they should bring his tefillin to his bed. They brought them to him. He removed them from their satchel, kissed them with affection, and repeated the motion. Then he withdrew the Rabbenu

Tam tefillin from the satchel and kissed them, and opened in a trembling and uneven voice:

> *To Thee my Lord, my yearning,*
> *In Thee, my faith, my affection,*
> *My mind, my guts, my being,*
> *My soul, my spirit, my direction.*
> *From Thee, my shape, my form,*
> *My breath, my strength, my feet.*
> *My refuge, haven in a storm,*
> *To Thee I turn when I entreat,*
> *Like a newborn with my sighs.*
> *To Thee I turn with my cries,*
> *Heal the affliction of my eyes.*

At that moment Ezra felt his heart fill with love; there seemed to be a river of tears flowing down Haham Pinto's cheeks. He had once heard from Haham Pinto that the moment of death is the moment filled with the greatest longing and yearning, for when the soul leaves the body it fills with light, as Scripture suggests, *Thou takest away their breath, they die.*

Rafael HaMekhaven joined the singing of the melody. Slowly but surely they all followed suit and continued the hymn:

> *In Thee I trust,*
> *On Thee I hang my every breath,*
> *Until I return to the dust and even after death.*
> *Filled with fear, plagued by ever growing terror,*
> *The moment I recall before Thee all my error*
> *I stand before Thee naked. How can I respond?*
> *My lies clamor first, nothing lies beyond*
> *My day of judgment before Thee arrived*
> *Thy ruling I dread, no hope survives*
> *Who can stand before Thee, who in my stead?*
> *How to justify myself before the One I dread?*

The group recited the hymn, gazing unceasingly at the Haham's face. The color of his cheeks turned from bright red to a pale white, all of a sudden they would flush and only a moment later they had the yellow pallor of an old Torah scroll. Haham Kahanof motioned for any who were priests to leave the room. They exited. Those who remained kept totally silent. Only Haham Rafael HaMekhaven continued in a hushed tone, and Haham Pinto, his lips moving, his eyes closed, seemed to be repeating after him:

> *On the day when I am gathered in,*
> *The day when I to meet Thee go,*
> *Accept my Lord my conduct so,*
> *And grant to me my just reward*
> *For those that follow Thee, O Lord.*

> *Send to me Thine angels of grace;*
> *Let them towards me quickly race.*
> *With one accord they welcome me,*
> *And greet me as I come to Thee.*
> *Before Thee may the light concealed*
> *Serve as my buckler and my shield.*
> *Beneath the shelter of Thy wing*
> *May I forever to Thee cling.*

Suddenly the Haham put his head down, as if he were about to sleep. The doctor stood in the doorway, looking at the group singing hymns together with the patient. In all his life, he had never seen a sight like this. He signaled to everyone to leave the room. As they did so, Haham Pinto opened his eyes for a moment and motioned for three of them to remain at his bedside: Haham Ventura, who delivered sermons during the Days of Repentance before the sounding of the shofar; Haham Menashe, who recited the prayers of Rav Alfiah to conclude the public fasts on the Mondays and Thursdays of the weeks when the first half of Exodus is read; and Ezra Siman Tov, the launderer.

Haham Yosef Pinto asked Haham Menashe to help him recite the Great Confession of Rabbenu Nissim, traditionally recited on the Day of Atonement:

> *Master of the Universe, first, I have neither a response to utter nor the impudence to raise my head. For my sins are beyond me, like a great burden I cannot bear. My iniquities are too many to be counted, my transgressions are beyond tally. I am ashamed of my sins, embarrassed by my wrongdoings, humiliated by my offenses, disgraced like a thief caught in the breach. With what shall I approach thee to request forgiveness, pardon, and absolution? What am I? What is my life? I am like chaff before a flame, like dry tinder before a fire, base metal coated with silver, vanity of vanities, all is vanity. Master of the Universe, Thy courts of true justice are not like the courts of mortals of flesh and blood. For in the courts of mortals one man sues another for payment and accompanies him to the judge; if he protests his innocence, he retains his money; if he admits his guilt, he must pay. But Thy court of true justice is not so; if man protests his innocence, woe unto him and woe unto his soul; if he admits his guilt, Thou hast mercy upon him.*

He continued and recited the whole confession in alphabetical order, from the beginning, We have trespassed, we have dealt treacherously, until We have gone astray, we have led others astray.

Afterwards, Haham Pinto asked Haham Ventura to approach and relayed in an undertone a few instructions for the care of his body after his death.

Finally, he called Ezra Siman Tov. Haham Pinto turned to him, and Ezra lowered his ear to his mouth. "Ezra, you should know that in my youth I had a pure heart and a simple soul. I did not know of crookedness. Much Torah have I learned from my rabbis and my teachers, even more from my colleagues, but the most from my students; the more I learned the more I sought a pure heart and a simple soul, such as I had in my youth." He wept and said, "May my end be like my beginning." He continued, "King David said at the end of the Psalm *Blessed are the Pure of Path, 'wandering like a lost sheep, search for Thy servant.'* If a man feels himself astray like a lost sheep, he should entreat the Shepherd to search for him." He continued to whisper, and finally he said: "The day will come when you will need these words. But now a blessing for you." He rested his hand on Ezra's head and blessed him with the priestly blessing, *May the Lord bless thee and protect thee! May the Lord shine His face upon thee and be gracious to thee! May the Lord lift up His countenance upon thee and grant thee..."*

The entire time Haham Ventura had been looking at Haham Pinto's face. He was not able to finish the final word of the blessing, *Peace,* before Haham Ventura hurried to recite the *Shema* in a loud voice.

The angels above overcame the great ones below. The Holy Ark was taken into captivity. Throngs filled the streets around the Zoharei Hamah Synagogue.

Haham Elijah Raful began in a sobbing voice:

Away have passed those we could trust
Bravery belonged to them from their good deeds
Calmly they had strength in facing evil
Delaying decrees and their consequence
Eternally our defense
Fighting anger with their words, their
Great prayers overcame bitterness
Heights scaled by their entreaties
Immediately Thou answered their knowing prayer
Judgment deferred, Thou showed them the
Kindness of a father to a son,
Leaving them never empty,
Many are our sins and so
None of the great ones remain
Off to their rest they journeyed,
Problems only remain

> *Quietly we seek those already perished*
> *Ready to face evil*
> *Strong enough to seek Thee*
> *They are dead and gone*
> *Unceasingly we wandered the world*
> *Verily none could fill their place.*

Ezra stood in a corner and tears poured down his face. The speakers delivered eulogies in praise of the departed one and words of rebuke for the newly orphaned generation. He heard but could not listen. The lines that Haham Raful had uttered kept ringing in his ears: *Off to their rest they journeyed, Problems only remain. Unceasingly we wandered the world, Verily none could fill their place.* Many images appeared before him. He wandered the world seeking a replacement he could not find, walking and drifting like a stray sheep. He tried desperately to conjure in his mind an image of the Haham as a healthy man in the prime of life, but could not.

Throughout the time the speakers were delivering eulogies for Haham Pinto, bulldozers were digging up the streets next to Mahane Yehudah and huge jackhammers were breaking up the stones. The people strained to hear the eulogies but the sounds of hammers and drills distracted them.

Chapter sixteen

In which we take leave of the eulogies and the construction and recount Ezra's pain.

The next day Ezra rose early, as he was wont to do, and went to the Zoharei Hamah Synagogue. Haham Pinto's place remained empty and the service had an element of glory, of majesty, and of splendor. It felt like the prayer during the week of the fast of the Ninth of Av. Only at the end of the service did Ezra realize that he had not watched the dawning of the day when reciting the blessing on the Heavenly Luminaries. After prayers, when they all sat down at the table to study the *Hok L'Yisrael*, each word reminded them of the Haham. They began to read a verse with its Aramaic translation and one of them remarked: "So I once heard from Haham Pinto." At the mere mention of his name they all immediately stood up out of respect for the Haham. Others began to quote his teachings. "Thus Haham Pinto explained this passage to us," said one. "No he interpreted it this way," replied another. "Actually he said neither the one nor the other, but recounted a parable," a third claimed.

Only Ezra was silent. He stared at the book and images

appeared to him in his head. With all his strength he tried to recall the image of the Haham's face, but was unsuccessful. He could not understand why. Each time he caught a glimpse of another part of the Haham's face, but could never see the entire image. When he tried to recall the Haham's utterances, he could not remember them. He had heard hundreds of teachings from him over the course of his life but not a single one appeared to him. All he could feel was his forehead aflame with the heat of Haham Pinto's hands when he recited the priestly blessing.

When he returned home later that morning and tasted the warm *Sahlep* that Madame Sarah had waiting for him, he put it down immediately. He put his head between his hands and was silent. Madame Sarah was silent too. After a few moments, he rose, took his leave of her, and went to work.

The bulldozers had torn up the street and dug out a sort of trench between the street on one side and the stores on the other. The entrance to every store was filled with dust and debris. The storeowners had laid planks and boards across the trench so they and their customers could come and go. Ezra skipped over a plank in order to reach the laundry, stumbled and fell. His clothes were soiled with dust. Prosper Azulai was standing in the entrance to his store, forcefully hitting a hammer against the twisted faucet of a Sabbath kettle which refused to straighten out. He hurried to give Ezra a hand, lifted him out of the ditch, and helped him wipe the dust off his clothing. "It's nothing," Ezra said, "It's nothing, may it atone for my sins, a man only bruises himself on this earth, if it has already been proclaimed in heaven. This too is for the best."

"What best? Who is this good for? Maybe for the contractors or the great commercial buildings that will be built here, but as for us, they are destroying everything," said Prosper, continuing to bang his hammer against the kettle in an attempt to set the crooked faucet straight. "Everything is already ruined, for the past week no one has come into the store. That's it, it's over, in another couple of weeks every shop will be closed. What will be, Ezra? What's going to happen to us?" Ezra gazed at Prosper's worried face as if he were searching for a parable or a pleasant story to comfort him, but he could find nothing. He was silent.

Ezra entered the laundry. He found Kaduri sitting there. No one had ever gotten to work before him. He looked at his watch and saw he was three minutes late. Ezra had never arrived late to work, not even a moment, and had never left work early, not for anything in the world. He had once heard Haham Pinto tell of Abba Hilkiah the son of Honi the Circle Drawer. When the world was in need of rain, the sages used to dispatch emissaries to him asking for his prayers. Once, the two scholars they sent for him found him hoeing in a field. They called out to him in greeting, but he did not respond. When they went to his home in the evening and asked why he had not responded to their greeting, he replied to them, "So as not to neglect my master's work." Ezra had also heard from the Haham that the sages scarcely allowed the craftsmen of Jerusalem to stand up and greet the pilgrims to the city. His face filled with anguish; he was distressed that he had stolen his employer's time. Kaduri saw he was filled with pain, looked at the clock, glanced at his dusty clothing, and said, "Forget it, Ezra, forget it. In any case, there's not much work to do."

He put his hand on Ezra's shoulder, showed him a registered letter with red lines and several signatures, and said to him, "Ezra, in another three weeks we are closing up. Already we are not receiving any clothing to clean. We will clean whatever we have here and return it to the customers."

"This too is for the best," Ezra replied.

Yehezkel Kaduri continued. "A lawyer came to speak with me. Maitre Hasson Zarfati. He said that in a few months they will send us the compensatory payments, and then we will divide them up among everyone."

Ezra folded a prayer shawl, taking great care to straighten out the folds and holding it tightly. "Yes," Ezra replied, "so I once heard from Haham Pinto, who used to say, why does a man worry about money rather than time, for money doesn't help, but time..." He tried to finish the thought but had forgotten the conclusion. He struggled to remember but was unsuccessful.

"Don't worry," Yehezkel reassured him, "don't worry, this too is for the best."

"In any case," Ezra exclaimed, "I will finally have the time to do all the things I have always wanted to do, like participate in every public fast day on the Mondays and Thursdays of the weeks when we read the first half of Exodus, or sit in the synagogue every day and read the entire book of Psalms three times. Every year I have wanted to do so. It pained me greatly that work prevented me and I was unable. From now on I will have time."

"Yes," continued Ezra, seemingly reinvigorated, "now I can do what I was never able to do, on Mondays I can go and attend Haham Pinto's sermon..." Suddenly he realized, he fell silent and sighed. He continued vigorously folding the prayer shawl, straightening its creases, and a single tear trickled down his cheek.

Rumors spread throughout Mahane Yehudah. They claimed that the digging would extend from the streets into the actual neighborhood itself. Some said that rich Americans fancied the beauty of the neighborhood, and its location in the center of Jerusalem, and wanted to purchase the old houses and build beautiful villas in their place. Others claimed they were planning to build tall buildings for commercial offices and large hotels that would obstruct the sunlight from the small houses. Contractors, surveyors, appraisers, and brokers appeared throughout the neighborhood. The residents gathered in the afternoons to exchange gossip, advisers dispensed their advice, the greedy calculated how much they could earn from the sale of their small house, and up to what point it was worth refusing to sell in order to raise the price. Someone told a story about a man in the shantytown: when they wanted to pave a wide road through his property on the corner of Betzalel Street, they negotiated with him and offered him huge sums of money for his house, but he refused; they persisted and made an even greater offer, but he still wanted more. In the end, they by-passed his house and he lost the entire offer. Pessimists predicted the worst, as they were wont to do, while comforters attempted to offer consolation.

Ezra Siman Tov's children also worried. Those in the know

informed them that right next to their father's home they were planning to build a twelve-story office building that would block their sun. They knew how much Ezra Siman Tov and Madame Sarah loved their small house and their bright verandah surrounded by potted plants and pickled vegetables, which was drenched with sunlight the entire winter.

One night all the children convened for a meeting in the home of the eldest brother. They discussed the matter at length, and concluded that since Kaduri's laundry was closing, and their father would no longer have work in Jerusalem, and since both parents were getting older and had no one to take care of them, because none of the children lived in Jerusalem, and because a huge office building was being built right next to their home anyway, it might make sense to sell the small home to one of the brokers and buy their parents a spacious home next to one of their children in Netanya.

Finally, they resolved to wait a few more weeks until they could present the matter to their parents, and following the well-known proverb they decided to approach their mother while their father attended the afternoon prayer at the Zoharei Hamah Synagogue and propose the idea to her. In the meantime they assigned one of the brothers to inquire with a couple of brokers about how much they could get for the house, and another brother to find an appropriate house in Netanya. And they told him to make sure to find a house next door to a synagogue with daily prayers.

When the day arrived they approached their mother at the time of the afternoon prayer. As soon as they entered the house she greeted them and cast a concerned glance at the setting sun in the west, saying, "Go to afternoon prayers, sunset is almost upon us, you may still be able to recite prayers at one of the later services. When you come home afterwards, then we can talk."

"We prayed already," they hastened to respond.

Their mother went into the kitchen and began to arrange delicacies. She always knew what each of her children loved to eat and prepared it for him. One liked hot food, another baked goods; one relished cucumbers preserved in brine as well as the small, pink eggplants she had pickled herself; another savored date and rose-petal jam and hazelnuts coated in honey; another the brittle sesame cookies she kept hidden in the flowered tin can. She looked at their faces, saw they were perplexed, but knew not how this day differed from any other or why they had all turned up all of a sudden. Since they said nothing, she did not ask. They spoke about this, that, and the other and stayed silent for much of the time.

They did not know what to say or how to say it. Each one looked at the other, waiting for him to begin. Suddenly they heard a loud noise from one of the tractors working next to the house. One of them began, "Mother, how much noise these machines make!"

Madame Sarah stood up and shut the window. "If the noise bothers you, I'll close the window."

"Does the noise not disturb you too?" The brothers chorused in response.

"Us?" Madame Sarah asked in astonishment, "Why should it bother us? The world is full of many noises, some pleasant, others less so, and we have trained our ears to hear what we want to hear and to ignore what we don't want to hear. The world is full of many sights, and our eyes are accustomed to see only what we want them to see. A man is master of his own body, your father always says in the name of the late Haham Pinto, and he decides who and what he allows to enter and who and what he does not."

"Mother, Mother, this is why we have come to talk to you. Tall buildings are being built next door and we are worried about you. They will obstruct the sunlight and make the pleasant air of Jerusalem unhealthy. We were thinking, maybe you would consider the possibility of coming to live in another city, near one of us. They have already closed the laundry, Haham Pinto has died recently, and they are also saying that Haham Kahanof is moving to Petah Tikvah to be near one of his children, and also...and also—"

Madame Sarah waved her hand in refusal. "Well," she said. "Very well. You have done well to come when your father is not at home. How much pain it would cause him to hear all of you! Is it not enough that he is plagued by the memory of his late teacher, Haham

Pinto, who does not leave his thoughts for even a moment, neither day nor night, that you have come to increase his anguish? What has gotten into you, that we should leave Jerusalem? Your father and I leave Jerusalem? Have you all lost your minds, heaven forbid? We should leave Jerusalem? You say they will darken our sunlight? Jerusalem light does not come from the sun. It is the light of the Divine Presence, and it is impossible to darken it. Where should we go? To a city without any light at all? They will obstruct our view from the window, you say, and our air will be unhealthy? Jerusalem air does not come through the windows. It is pure air, purified by the holiness of Jerusalem. They are shutting Kaduri's laundry? This too is for the best. Certainly this will allow your father to spend more of his time studying Torah, as he has wanted to do his entire life. Banish the worry from your hearts. Our days are pleasant and sweet in Jerusalem. We do not seek grand things. We do not want a spacious house. Our small apartment is perfect for us and we are perfect for it. It is enough that we have been worthy to tread the streets of Jerusalem for sixty years."

The brothers understood there was nothing more for them to say, and they carried on discussing other things.

On every Sabbath during the month following Haham Pinto's death a memorial service was held in the Zoharei Hamah Synagogue. Three preachers delivered sermons. Each time the synagogue was filled with rabbis, *avrechim*, and common folk who came out of respect for the Haham and the mourners. Ezra sat among them and listened to the words of Torah, to ethical rebuke and reproach, parables and interpretations, numerologies and acrostics, exegesis of Scripture and legal casuistry, innovations in legal rulings, and messages of comfort and yearning for the coming redemption. The synagogue was filled with Torah. Although no Haham attracted his heart the way Haham Pinto had, nevertheless, the abundance of Torah, the many scholars, the public anguish over the loss, the words of comfort offered, the stories recounted about the Haham, all these took his mind off the mourning.

When the month was over, the memorial services ended. On the following Sabbath, Ezra wanted to hear a sermon, as he had for the past fifty years. His feet carried him of their own accord to the Zoharei Hamah Synagogue, but when he arrived he found only a few elderly men reciting psalms. Not wanting to interrupt their reading, they signaled to him with their hands that there was no sermon that Sabbath. It had never even occurred to Ezra that a Sabbath could pass without a sermon. Much as there could be no Sabbath without the sanctification of wine, the three meals accompanied by two loaves of bread, the hot stew, the songs, and the dawn hymns, there could be none without a sermon. But on that Sabbath there was no sermon at the Zoharei Hamah Synagogue. At the time Ezra did not know that at the end of the month of memorial services delivered for Haham Pinto the beadles of the synagogue had deliberated for many hours but could not agree on who would deliver the sermons in Haham Pinto's place. They argued bitterly over the issue. The elders wanted Haham Kahanof, the learned wanted to institute an in-depth lecture on Tractate Sabbath instead of the sermon, the young said that times had changed and tastes with them, that no one wanted to listen to parables, stories, sermons, or interpretations of the Torah based on rabbinic writings; they wanted something else, and they sought to bring in a young rabbi whose manner suited the new generation: A rabbi who would deliver a lecture on a contemporary issue in an eloquent fashion. Since they were not able to reach an agreement, the sermons were discontinued for the interim.

Ezra hurried to the Zikhron Kedoshim Synagogue and discovered a rabbi splitting hairs about recent rabbinic writings on a passage in Tractate Sabbath, but his words failed to penetrate Ezra's heart. He went to the Central Synagogue and heard a rabbi-professor lecturing on the parallels between a particular reflexive verb in Ugaritic, Aramaic, and the Holy Tongue, based on the latest findings in philological research. He wandered to the Bukharan quarter and found a group of Bukharan Jews wearing white clothing and women's sandals, listening to an *avrech* explicate a passage from the *Zohar*, but Ezra did not engage in mysticism. He walked to the Ahdut Yisrael Synagogue but found no one there. For fifty years Ezra had heard Haham Pinto's Sabbath sermon. The sermons had filled his soul, delighted him, taught him a way of living, and guided his life in the path of the just. That Sabbath Ezra did not hear a sermon. Ezra Siman Tov picked up the psalter and began to recite.

When he arrived home, Madame Sarah looked at him and saw his distress. "What happened, Ezra?" she asked. "Today is the Sabbath, and it is a received tradition that one cannot be distraught on the Sabbath, for it was given for delight."

"Yes, today is the Sabbath," he answered, "but the flavor of the Sabbath, the spice of the Sabbath is gone. This Sabbath I did not hear a sermon."

"Ezra," she replied soothingly, "don't you always tell me, *generations come and generations go, but the earth endures forever.*"

"Yes," he responded, "the earth may endure forever, but the land beneath me seems out of joint. Yesterday I heard from Haham Kahanof that the generations have changed. People no longer seek purity. They want something different. They pour scorn on the naiveté of the innocent old Jerusalemites. And they, the humble folk of Jerusalem, are fast disappearing. Don't you remember that even the spice sellers in the Mahane Yehudah market were just and upright, with bright countenances, men who rose early for prayers and remained in the house of study until late at night, and possessed genuine love of life? How purity poured over their faces as they cried out their wares to the tune of the dawn hymns on the eve of the holy Sabbath? Friday evening on Betzalel Street or Meyuhas Street the holiness was nearly palpable. But now it seems that even the streets of Jerusalem are changing. I heard that they are changing cantors at the Zoharei Hamah Synagogue as well. They want the younger cantors with strong pleasant voices who can sing solos to the latest tunes. They ridicule the older cantors whose voices are hoarse and husky. What do they know? Can this younger generation hear how much love for God and purity of soul is hidden in the hoarseness of Haham Selim's voice or the huskiness of Haham Raful's, how much beauty is in the thoughts to which they direct their minds during prayer? They want new rabbis. Rabbis who will speak their language. Have they any conception of the beauty of Haham Pinto's language, so pure that one never heard a single shameful word? Do they know that each interpretation he offered in his sermons not only served to explicate the sources themselves but penetrated to the very depths of those listening, who would immediately decide to correct their ways and refine their character? I myself did not know while Haham Pinto was still alive how much my soul was tied to him. Now that he has departed from this world, I am beginning to understand some of the things he said to me. It is true, they say that Jerusalem has many learned rabbis, erudite *avrechim*, scholars, mystics, but what can I do, their worlds are not mine. I hope my world will not disappear. At least our home is still here, its walls still soaked in the atmosphere of the Jerusalem of long ago. You are still here with me. And the book of Psalms has not changed. How great was the purity that David planted therein. My world remains immersed in each and every single psalm. When I read the psalms, the sermons of the Haham, his images, stories, and conduct appear before me. This too is for the best. So Haham Pinto once said to us, sometimes when He in heaven seeks a man, it seems as if the world is lost, but this is only because He is building a new and better world. At the time I didn't understand what he meant, and even now I do not know. But all that comes from Heaven comes for the better. This too is for the best, and good will come upon us. Good Sabbath Sarah, good Sabbath. Come, let us sit on the verandah like we usually do, and bask in the warm light of the Sabbath, let us read the midrash of the weekly portion and live our lives according to the words of the sages."

At the conclusion of that Sabbath, Ezra and Madame Sarah paid a visit to her great brother Doctor Tawil, as was their custom every week. After they had sung the songs of Elijah the Prophet, had tea together, and spoken of this and that, Doctor Tawil asked Ezra to recount a story, as he did every week at the conclusion of the Sabbath. Ezra was silent. Doctor Tawil waited for him, while editing a new article he had written on the verb patterns employed by the Nagid in his cycle of poems, *Son of Ecclesiastes*. Occasionally he would lift his eyes from the article, look at Ezra and say, "Ezra, do you remember a story told by Haham Menashe or Haham Betzalel?" Ezra was silent. Not a single story occurred to him. Doctor Tawil returned to his article, and Ezra sat beside him in silence. "Is something wrong today, Ezra?" said Doctor Tawil raising his eyes, "Does Jerusalem have no more stories? Have the wellsprings dried up?" Madame Sarah tried to hint to her brother to leave Ezra alone but he pretended not to notice. "Ezra," he continued, "can't you repeat a story you have already told me? It is impossible to begin the week without hearing a story. Perhaps you can recount to us a story told by the late Haham Pinto, or one of his parables." Ezra struggled to remember either a story or a parable but could not. He tried to conjure the image of the Haham before him but failed.

Thus they continued sitting, Madame Sarah, who was talking with her sister-in-law, occasionally casting a worried glance at Ezra, Doctor Tawil immersed in his article, and Ezra Siman Tov sitting at his side in silence. After an hour they rose to take their leave as they did every Saturday night following the Sabbath. Doctor Tawil accompanied them to the door, his article in one hand and his editing pencil in the other. Ezra Siman Tov was standing at the door about to leave when he suddenly paused. He turned to Dr. Tawil, "Yes, yes, I remember a story that actually happened." Doctor Tawil put down his article and stared at Ezra. "A story that I heard in Zikhron Kedoshim about Rabbi Israel, the Baal Shem Tov," said Ezra Siman Tov. "I have heard that the Hasidim say it is fitting to recount stories about Rabbi Israel, the Baal Shem Tov, on the Saturday night after the Sabbath.

"Once, when the Baal Shem Tov sought to ascend to the Land of Israel, he, his daughter and Rabbi Zvi Sofer boarded a ship bound for Constantinople and arrived there on the eve of Passover without knowing a single soul. On the first day of the festival's intermediary days they booked passage on a ship headed for the Land of Israel and embarked on their voyage. For two whole days terrible tempests battered the boat to the point of ruin. On the third day the storm settled and they managed to land at a certain island. All the passengers disembarked in order to see the island and to stretch their limbs on dry land, even the Baal Shem Tov, his daughter, and Rabbi Zvi. After walking for a while on the island, they discovered they were lost and could not find their way back to the boat. Suddenly bandits fell upon them, tied them up with ropes, and began to sharpen their knives. Rabbi Zvi beseeched the Baal Shem Tov, 'Why does the master keep silent at a time like this? Let him perform a miracle to save us from this suffering as he always does!'

"'I do not know anything now, all my powers have been taken from me,' replied the Baal Shem Tov. 'Perhaps you yourself remember something that I taught you? Remind me!'

"'I too have forgotten everything and do not know anything,' answered Rabbi Zvi. 'I cannot remember a single thing. I can only recall the letters of the alphabet.'

"'If so, what are you waiting for?' the Baal Shem Tov screamed at him, 'tell them to me!' Rabbi Zvi began to recite: 'Aleph, bet, gimmel' and the Baal Shem Tov fervently repeated the letters in a towering voice, until his concentration and his many powers were restored to him. He directed his mind and suddenly an officer came with an entire regiment, apprehended the bandits, and released the prisoners. The Baal Shem Tov understood that heaven was preventing him from ascending to the Land of Israel and returned home."

The next day, Sunday, after the morning prayer and the recitation of the *Hok L'Yisrael*, Ezra Siman Tov tarried in the Zoharei Hamah Synagogue and did not hasten to fold his tefillin. He lingered at the table and leafed through a book of sermons he had found. Why should he hurry? That week Kaduri's laundry had closed.

On the way home, he realized he was not going about his day like a man weighed down by his work. From then on he would not be so encumbered. The entire day was before him. His thoughts occupied him. Many days had he spent dreaming of the time when he could always study Torah. Now, when that time had actually come, he could not set his mind at ease.

Before he arrived at his house, he saw a man coming towards him. His face was the face of a Jerusalem Sephardi, his dress the dress of an Ashkenazi Hasid; long curling sidelocks, a tattered *kapota*, and dark sad eyes. A large wet towel was draped over his shoulders and his prayer shawl and tefillin were tucked under his arms. He looked familiar. But before he could even think, the Hasid approached him: "Ezra, Ezra, I haven't seen you for such a long time. Not since you came with me to the forest. Ezra, always be happy! Always! One should only be happy. There is a great Father in heaven. No need to give up on the world at all. No despair, no sadness, only great happiness. Come Ezra, let's dance for our Father in heaven. I must have great merit to meet you first thing in the morning. It is great sign to meet Ezra Siman Tov."

The Hasid gazed into Ezra's eyes as if he were searching for something. "Ezra, Ezra," he called, "I am searching for the light, the light in your eyes. Where is the light that once lit up your face? Where is it?" He seized Ezra by the shoulders and shook him. "One should only be happy. There is absolutely no despair in the world."

"Certainly not," Ezra replied. "There is certainly no despair. None at all."

Ezra continued on his way home. After he had eaten breakfast, he stood up and said, "I am going to study Torah."

In truth it would have been fitting to ask him what he would study, with whom, how, where; but Madame Sarah, as usual, did not ask many questions. She only looked at him and said, "May the Lord be with you." Ezra left the house and began walking, but knew not where to go. His feet took him of their own accord to Jaffa Road. From a distance he could see the laundry. While debating whether or not to go any nearer, he found he had already taken himself there. As he realized where he was standing, he peered inside. The laundry was empty, filled with dust, rubble, and the leftover rubbish from the machines. He could still make out a single crumpled dress lying on an ironing board as well as two shirts on the floor. Two great white chalk marks coated the plate-glass window that opened on to the street. Prosper's small shop was also closed. Tin shutters lay in front of the doorway, coated with the same white chalk marks. In front of the shutters someone had set up a table and was selling lottery tickets.

Ezra kept walking on Jaffa Road immersed in his thoughts. As he proceeded he saw Reb Moishe Dovid coming towards him, clasping a large volume of the Talmud in his hands. Ezra fixed his eyes on the ground in an attempt to avoid being seen, but Reb Moishe Dovid called out in a loud voice, "Ezra, good morning." Quietly, Ezra mumbled a response and silently prayed that he would not be detained in conversation. "Ezra, Ezra," cried Reb Moishe Dovid, "where are you headed? I heard Kaduri shut the laundry, that they are widening the street and building a great new shopping center." Dumbfounded, Ezra had no idea what to respond.

"Yes," he said, "the laundry was shut."

"What will all the workers do now?" Reb Moishe Dovid continued, "I bet they will all receive hefty compensation. And you, what will you do?" Ezra was silent. "Do you want to join me?" Reb Moishe Dovid suddenly asked. "I am on my way to the Ahdut Yisrael Synagogue. Right now I am in the middle of a very difficult passage that requires tremendous concentration. There not a soul can disturb me. Come with me."

Ezra went along. They entered the synagogue. No one was there. Ezra approached the ark and kissed the curtain covering it. Reb Moishe Dovid sat down next to the long table, opened the volume of the Talmud, and began to read the passage from the very beginning in a didactic tone, as if he were giving someone a lesson, asking rhetorical questions, explaining a particular problem, adducing proofs and refutations from the Ancients and the Moderns. Ezra sat beside him, looking at him and listening. Several hours later Reb Moishe Dovid's face lit up and he said, "The passage finally makes sense! Maimonides' different decisions have been reconciled; the words of the Tosafot are clear; those of Rabbenu Asher are lucid, and the legal decision in the *Four Pillars* is as white and pure as a summer dress. All thanks to you, Ezra," he exclaimed joyfully. "Thanks to you. Many days I have labored over this passage, but I could not find an explanation until today."

Ezra was silent. He kissed the volume of the Talmud as he shut it. He had great love for the Torah but he had not understood a word of what Reb Moishe Dovid had taught him. He could neither understand what had bothered Reb Moishe Dovid nor how he had resolved his dilemma; why Abraham ben David of Posquières had been so infuriated in his gloss to Maimonides' code or how Joseph Karo appeased his wrath three hundred years later. He had once heard Haham Pinto interpret the second verse of the Psalms, *The Torah of the Lord is his delight and he studies his Torah day and night*, saying that at first it is God's Torah; only after one has labored does it becomes his own. Ezra said to himself, "This is the Torah of my friend Reb Moishe Dovid, for he has worked for it, but it is not my own."

"If you'd like," Reb Moishe Dovid turned to him, "you can come to study with me tomorrow, and we can discuss another passage." Reb Moishe Dovid did not wait for a response but continued on his way. Ezra went to the bookshelf, reached for a psalter, and began to read the portion allocated for the first day of the week.

After he had finished the daily reading, he went to the market. Not tarrying there long, he quickly purchased his fruits and vegetables before going to the Zoharei Hamah Synagogue for the early recitation of the afternoon prayer. After the service he stayed for Haham Kahanof's class on halakha in *The Ben Ish Hai*. When the class ended someone took out a bottle of spirits and some sweets in order to bid farewell to Haham Kahanof, who had taught Torah at the synagogue for forty years, day after day, but was moving to Petah Tikvah to live with his son. The man proposed a toast that he should continue to draw crowds of people to the Torah and instruct them to fear Heaven, and recited the verse from Psalms, *In old age they still produce fruit, they are full of sap and freshness*. Another man rose and composed numerologies using the letters of Haham Kahanof's name. Finally, the Haham himself delivered a short address. At the end, before they recited the evening prayer, the beadle added that due to the recent decision of the communal board, the classes on *The Son of the Living* would no longer continue; henceforth, a group of younger rabbis would deliver classes on a rotating basis. They planned to deal with subjects in Jewish law related to modern life, contemporary issues; the entire community was invited to attend.

Ezra had known Haham Kahanof was planning to move but had not realized that day was to be his last. He approached the Haham and kissed his hand. Haham Kahanof placed his hand on his head and blessed him. Ezra looked at him and thought he could see tears in his eyes. Before they parted the Haham said: "Ezra, there will probably be some people in Petah Tikvah who want a class on *The Ben Ish Hai* between the afternoon and evening prayers, don't you think so?"

Ezra stood silently, gazing lovingly at the Haham.

When Ezra arrived home after the evening prayer, he found his great brother-in-law, Doctor Tawil, waiting for him. He invited him to an important conference on the poems of Yehudah HaLevi at the university. Throughout the day the greatest scholars of medieval Hebrew poetry would deliver lectures on his poems. He too planned to lecture about his most recent article, and now that Ezra finally had time on his hands he would be able to learn from the world of scholarship. Ezra Siman Tov knew the poems of Yehudah HaLevi from the hymns he sang at his in-law's on the Sabbath, as well as those bearing the acrostic Yehudah, recited on the Days of Awe, and the poem which began 'O Lord thy Mercy,' recited on the Sabbath of Remembrance every year before the additional morning service, and *The day when the dry land...* sung on the seventh day of Passover and at feasts of circumcision, for it includes the verse, *Those who enter Thy covenant sealed, from the womb in which they are circumcised.* Ezra Siman Tov asked his great brother-in-law if the conference would include a recital of the poems sung by the great cantors. Doctor Tawil smiled condescendingly and replied: "It is a scholarly conference at the Hebrew University, not an evening of song in Mahane Yehudah. This is not a gathering of simpletons, but one for scholars and men of letters. Important professors will examine the meter and diction of different poems, and they may also discuss certain recently dis-covered passages whose attribution to HaLevi has been questioned." Ezra nodded his head, as if to say, I never refuse the request of my friends, if you'd like I will come and listen.

Ezra was unaware that Doctor Tawil's invitation to the important conference was not a coincidence, just as Reb Moishe Dovid did not simply happen upon him in the street and invite him to study. Madame Sarah had been worried about Ezra. She saw the expression on his face, knew what transpired in his soul, and tried to arrange these meetings for him. She had thought they might assuage his pain. Ezra passed his time listening to lectures that did not penetrate his soul; occasionally he even went to listen to sermons by scholars that failed to set his mind at ease; but most of his time he spent alone in the synagogue, reading the weekly portion, the Aramaic translation, the *Hok L'Yisrael*, and above all the psalms. When he returned home he saw that the builders digging near his house had dug even deeper. Wooden scaffolding protruded over their verandah and obstructed their sunlight. Dust and muck filled the air. The aroma of the herbs in the flowerpots along the verandah, usually green and refreshing, had withered away. Their color had faded. In those days Ezra seemed to be searching for something, although he was unsure what. Sorrow and anguish descended upon him. Images appeared along with the sorrow. Images he thought he had banished many years ago stood before him, confounding him.

Chapter seventeen

The Dawning of the Day.

One day while sitting at his table, Ezra took his head between his hands and cried out in anguish. His wife saw him. She approached and said, "Ezra." He was silent. "Ezra," she repeated in a trembling voice, "did something remind you of her?" But he remained silent. He knew she understood. She always knew the secrets of his heart. Tears welled up in her eyes.

Ever since the misfortune had occurred to their daughter, the misfortune that shook all Jerusalem, they had never mentioned it in their home, neither explicitly nor implicitly. It seemed to have been forgotten. Now with the return of Ezra's sorrow, her image appeared before him and filled him with longing. Thoughts plagued him relentlessly. Where was she? What had happened to her? Wherever he went her image followed him. He could see her innocence, and O what innocence! He recalled her compassion, and such compassion! Her entire being was filled with love. When she was a baby, everyone was amazed how similar she was to her father. As a child they said she took after him in her purity. Her eyes always dreaming. Ezra remembered how much her mother worried about her naiveté.

How she used to volunteer to feed the sick in the local hospitals. Not a single chore was too difficult for her. She used to feed the gravely ill, wash them, and make their beds. The compassionate nurses of all the hospitals knew her. She was called to feed and care for the most embittered patients who refused to be fed and cared for by anyone else. But when they saw her from afar, their faces lit up.

Ezra remembered how one of the elders of the Zoharei Hamah Synagogue had warned him that his wife had seen Ezra's daughter tending to the sick in the French Hospital; that it seemed dangerous, and certain things had already happened. But he had not understood why he was being warned, what kind of danger there could be, what could possibly happen to her. He never knew what stood behind the bronze green doors that were always shut. He only knew there were very ill patients. From time to time people insinuated that he should forbid his daughter from going there. But he had not understood, until suddenly the catastrophe occurred and she disappeared as if the ground had swallowed her up.

No one could say where she went. Rumors circulated throughout Jerusalem and grim allusions were made. But Ezra and his wife heard nothing and could not understand what had happened. What had they not done during those days? How many tears had they shed, how many worlds did they shake, crying, entreating, and pleading. They waited for hours at the French Hospital in front of the heavy green doors until someone opened a small window. A clerk told them the hospital had no information and knew nothing. Their daughter was not registered as an employee and they had nothing to say. Ezra cried out, "But everyone knows that she used to volunteer here every day, helping you with your work."

"Yes," the clerk responded, "it's true that from time to time good young girls come and assist with the feeding of the sick, but they are already of age and do what they do of their own volition, and they are not the responsibility of the hospital."

A nurse dressed in white motioned to them and seemed to be saying something with her hand but they could not understand what she was trying to tell them, and when they tried to follow her she disappeared into one of the rooms. They looked for her but could not find her. All the rooms looked the same, all the nurses had their lips sealed, staring at Ezra as if he was disturbing their important work and unable to understand what he wanted from them. Day after day he and Madame Sarah went and waited in front of the green bronze doors only to return empty-handed.

One of the elders of the Zoharei Hamah Synagogue turned to Ezra one morning: "I don't know if this has anything to do with your daughter, but I heard that in the French Hospital there were several men who tried to induce young Jewish women to convert." Someone else hinted to him that he heard from a person who had a sick relative in the French Hospital that he had seen her in the company of a French friar who worked in the hospital and was trying to draw closer to her. But even these reports did not penetrate Ezra's heart and he could not understand their relevance to him. Until the letter arrived:

Dearest Mother and Father:

I cannot explain to you what happened. I just want to tell you that I followed my heart, and I am in a world filled with love, light, and compassion. Please do not worry about me. I am well. Do not seek me, for you will not find me.

She had written many other things that Ezra did not understand. At first they rejoiced that she was still alive. Later they were filled with shame, worry, and pain. Ezra went to show the letter to his great brother-in-law, Doctor Tawil. He read the letter in its entirety; his face grew pale, and he fell silent. Finally, when he saw Ezra and Sarah's pleading eyes, he lowered his gaze and said, "She is in a bad way. One of the friars in the French Hospital seduced her into following him and she did so. It appears that he was one of the missionaries. They say that there are several of them here in Jerusalem." Difficult days fell upon Ezra and Madame Sarah. All Jerusalem trembled because of the catastrophe of their daughter.

Ezra had not the strength to reflect on those days. It was as if he had erased them from his life. But what could he do now, for sadness had struck, the thoughts came on their own, his anguish was filled with his reflections, her image came and went before him, first in the house, then in the synagogue, in his dreams, as he walked; at times she was entreating him, others hiding from him; now crying, then laughing; first like a spoilt child before her father, then like a young girl running in the fields. Madame Sarah gazed at him and knew from the look on his face that he was thinking about her; tears welled up in her eyes.

One night during the evening prayer, Ezra, with his head buried in the prayer-book *The Complete Prayer of the Just*, published by Salah Mansour on Meyuhas Street in Mahane Yehudah, saw Haham Pinto's image appear between the black letters of the page, as if he were standing before him. Ever since the day of his passing, Ezra had not been able to see his image, either asleep or awake. But now he appeared with great clarity, resting his hands upon Ezra's head and blessing him.

That same night Ezra heard a knock at his door. When he opened the door he was taken aback. In the doorway stood Rahamim Kalifa the fiddler. For many years, week after week, Ezra had visited Rahamim, but Rahamim had rarely visited his house. Rahamim stood lingering in the doorway, his violin tucked under his arm, bow in hand and dark glasses over his eyes. Ezra had not seen him for a long time. The last time had been at the *Tikkun Karet* on his birthday at his home. That night when Rahamim took his leave, he had said he needed to leave Jerusalem in order to accompany the doctor who was going to administer daily treatments to his eye.

"Welcome Rahamim," Ezra cried out in astonishment, "Welcome. How were you able to come here all by yourself? Your treatment must surely have progressed since we last saw each other."

"*Blessed is the one who recompenses those in need, and performs wonders, blessed is He and blessed is His name,*" replied Rahamim, "and blessed are those here to receive me. Yesterday I returned home. Today my friend the writer paid a visit to me and told me to come to you. I don't know who informed him of my return to Jerusalem nor do I know what he meant, but I had been meaning to visit you in any case. I have a favor to request."

Ezra invited him inside. Madame Sarah served tea and fresh *ka'ak*. "Ezra," Rahamim began, "the time has not yet come for me to recount to you all that I have been through. I shall only say that through God's kindness I can begin to read large-print letters. They prepared unique glasses for the one eye the doctor saved with his new operation. Ezra, I have but one request of you: I want you to teach me Torah. For many years I have only been able to hear and play music; now I want to read and study. I am sure that you don't have a lot of time for me, but please, do not refuse my request. I promise not to burden you unnecessarily."

Ezra was stunned. In his entire life no one had ever asked him to teach Torah. "Me? That I should teach Torah to you?" Ezra asked, bewildered. "I have a lot of time, I will try to fulfill your request and help you with all that you might need, but that I should teach you Torah? What has gotten into you, Rahamim? Jerusalem is a city filled with scholars and writers! Have you not found anyone in the entire city of Jerusalem to teach you Torah apart from Ezra Siman Tov the launderer?"

Rahamim pleaded with him. "Ezra, didn't you once tell me in the name of Haham Pinto, that Aaron and his sons received the priestly crown, David and his sons the royal crown, but the crown of Torah lies there for whoever rises up to take hold of it? And we, are we not worthy enough to study Torah? What does it matter to you, we will study together, understand what we can; for whatever we don't understand we will consult the commentaries; what the commentaries do not explain we will ask someone else. Please, this is my request. My heart tells me that only with you can I study Torah. One cannot learn from just anyone."

Throughout his life Ezra had never refused anyone who made a request of him, and it did not occur to him to turn Rahamim down, even though he could not understand his request. They agreed to study every day for several hours and divide their time into three parts: a third Scripture, a third Mishnah and Halakha, and a third ethics and homilies. They decided to study in a small corner in the back of the Zoharei Hamah Synagogue. It was a narrow room with paint peeling from the walls. A miniature ark stood in the center of the room with the verse *I have set the Lord before me forever* upon it. Occasionally a small minyan gathered in the room for the afternoon service, but it was empty for most of the day except for one humble *avrech* who sat at a desk writing his own interpretations to the Talmud. They say he had studied in the Yeshiva and academy for many years; now he was writing down his Talmudic interpretations so as not to forget them. They studied and he wrote. Both Ezra and Rahamim knew that all beginnings were difficult. They grasped little, leaving much not understood. When they understood something they rejoiced; when they didn't, they experienced frustration. Sometimes they read the text of the Talmud incorrectly and muddled the entire passage.

When the *avrech* heard them err, he did not reproach them for their mistakes, but raised his voice as he studied, as if by mere coincidence he happened to be studying the identical passage. When they heard him read the passage correctly, they amended their own reading and understood their mistakes. Occasionally when they did not understand something, they approached him. "Excuse us, sir; perhaps you could enlighten us about this issue..."

After listening to their question and identifying their mistake he would modestly respond: "Your reading is excellent, your ideas sound; but perhaps it should be read as follows, similar to your suggestion." The issues were clarified as he repeated the entire passage in his sweet style, explaining each question and answer, until the text was entirely clear. Finally he turned to them, after answering all of their doubts. "Do you see, together all three of us interpreted the passage and solved the problem." Then he would return to his writing. Thus they continued, day after day, happy with their lot. One day, after several weeks of studying, they realized they had discovered on their own a dilemma raised in Rashi's commentary. They rejoiced. On another occasion they understood the Mishnah precisely as the commentators interpreted it. At that moment no one could compare to the two of them. Ezra turned to his friend. "Rahamim, I remember Haham Pinto. When he departed I went to him to receive a blessing. He said to me then, 'Ezra, every man must say, the issue depends only upon me.' At the time I didn't understand what he meant. Now I do.'"

In those days Madame Sarah saw Ezra wait expectantly every morning to go study with Rahamim; when he returned home she saw the same color in his cheeks that they used to have when he returned from Haham Pinto's sermon. She sat on the verandah, wrapped in a shawl, cleaning each and every bit of dust and all the leaves that the construction workers had raised digging up the street, attempting to turn the leaves up to the light. A while later, she took Ezra by the hand and showed him how their plants had returned and a small flower had begun to bloom.

At the beginning Rahamim and Ezra did not discuss other things but immersed themselves entirely in their study. After several weeks, when they had habituated themselves to their study and to one another, Ezra occasionally remembered a homily, story, or sermon of Haham Pinto's and recounted it to Rahamim. From time to time, in moments of tranquility, he even recounted his own tales. As he told his own stories, the image of Haham Pinto appeared before him and a smile spread across his face, and he told the stories slowly and gracefully, Rahamim hanging upon his every word. One time Rahamim turned to him and said, "You recount such pleasant stories, you should write them down so they are not forgotten. The people of Jerusalem are dwindling, and who will tell their tales? Even their speech has already disappeared." Ezra nodded his head as the words entered his ears.

That same night, when he arrived home, he sat at the table, took out a notebook and wrote down the story he had recounted to Rahamim. He said to himself, "I will write just one story." As he was writing he was reminded of another story, and then of another. Stories that he had heard during sermons delivered at memorial services, at ceremonies celebrating the conclusion of a tractate in the Talmud; stories that he had recounted to Rahamim on Thursday night or to his brother-in-law Doctor Tawil. Ezra was neither a writer nor the son of a writer, neither a man of letters nor an imaginative storyteller. He was a simple man. But he knew how to tell a tale. What he heard, what he saw, what he felt, so he wrote. He wrote in a simple style, in the language spoken by the people of Jerusalem in Mahane Yehudah and the Bukharan Quarter, the Ades Synagogue and the Zoharei Hamah Synagogue, language filled with the grace of Jerusalem. The hours that he spent writing were very dear to him, and a particular sweetness filled his entire being. Often he felt in his heart what he was writing. He sat and wrote, with Madame Sarah at his side gazing at him. Sometimes she could see a ray of light illumine his face, that same light that filled his face when he returned from studying Talmud with Rahamim and she felt deep affection. Slowly but surely the stories gathered and the entire notebook filled up. He went and purchased another notebook and before long, a pile of notebooks filled with his stories lay on the table.

Thus Ezra and Rahamim studied for an entire year, laboring over the Torah. They were worthy to finish several tractates of the Mishnah and many laws became fluent in their mouths. They decided to convene a *Tikkun Karet* at the end of a year of study. They resolved to study for the entire night one Thursday. And so they did. While they were studying, the modest *avrech* sat behind them writing. Ezra approached him and said, "For an entire year you have helped us, but we have never been properly introduced to you." The *avrech* smiled, did not respond, and returned to his writing. After they had studied the entire night and the hour of dawn was upon them, Ezra and Rahamim went out to take in the pure air of Jerusalem and prepare themselves for prayer. Ezra cherished this hour, the hour before sunrise. Rahamim did too. As he was accustomed to do in moments of great emotion, Rahamim took his violin with him.

As they got up to leave the synagogue the *avrech* approached them and said, "My entire life I have lived among the scholars and I have never seen people study the Torah for its own sake like the two of you. May people like you become numerous in the house of Israel."

Ezra and Rahamim left the synagogue and went on their way

to the valley beneath the shantytown at the bottom of Betzalel Street; that same valley the lone wandering Hasidim of Jerusalem frequented when seeking divine union.

The two of them stood in the open field, breathing the crisp air, silently gazing at the horizon, careful not to disturb the tranquility. A few moments later they heard a voice in the distance. "Father, Father, I have returned to you. You are our Father. The Father of the entire world, My Father, Father, please forgive me, pardon me." The voice continued, growing stronger. "I have come back to you. In happiness, always in happiness. Without despair, never in despair. Here I have returned to you out of love. Father."

Ezra heard the voice, felt it in his heart, and his eyes filled with tears. The tears blurred his vision. What was this before him? Something like an image appeared through the tears. From afar, from the field. He struggled to make it out. He saw an image approaching in the darkness, with a knitted scarf on her shoulders, extremely pale, her eyes dreamy and innocent. The sun slowly began its ascent. And Ezra could hear her. He was sure he could hear her. The words were clear, entreating. The voice in the distance. "Father, father I have come back. Please, please, forgive me, pardon me. I have come back to you."

Ezra's entire being shuddered. The air in Jerusalem was chilly at that hour. Cold and pure. The horizon grew brighter. The dawning of the day. His head was spinning. The voice in his ears, "father, father, father."

The melody of the violin could be heard, as if from another world. It contained a hymn, a mystery, a fragment of holiness. As if it were praying. It descended to the very depths and released a sad buried sigh; then it ascended and ascended; a glimmer of happiness could be heard, and it continued its ascent, rejoicing, leaving the darkness behind as a ray of light broke through in the east. Like the dawning of the day. Like the dawning of the day.

About the Author

Haim Sabato

Haim Sabato, born in Cairo, Egypt, in 1952, descends from a long line of rabbis from Aleppo, Syria. His family had lived in Egypt for two generations, before moving to Israel when he was five. He served in the tank corps in the 1973 Yom Kippur War, and teaches in a yeshiva near Jerusalem, which he co-founded.

Sabato's first novel, *Emet Me'Aretz Titzmach*, translated as *Aleppo Tales*, appeared in 1997. His second novel, *Tiyum Kavanot*, *Adjusting Sights*, was awarded the prestigious Sapir Prize for Literature in 2000 and the Yitzchak Sadeh Prize for Literature in 2002. Both have been published in English by *The* Toby Press.

The fonts used in this book are from the Garamond family

Other works by Haim Sabato available from *The* Toby Press

Adjusting Sights
Aleppo Tales